BURNING

PREQUEL - AFTER THE THAW

TAMAR SLOAN
HEIDI CATHERINE

SEQUEL HOUSE

For K with love

AMITY

*R*emnants approaching! Remnants approaching!

The urgent voice over the speakers spears through Amity's sleep, and she's out of bed before her drowsy brain can keep up. With her heart pummeling at her ribs, she scrambles in the dark for her clothes, confused but alert all at once.

Slipping on her woven shoes, she blinks in the black, warm room.

Remnants are approaching.

Visits from these bedraggled clumps of humanity have become less and less common, but everyone knows exactly what they could mean for Askala.

Practically on automatic pilot, Amity scans the back of her hand over the sensor and the door of her small, bunk-like room whooshes open. Within seconds, she's running down the narrow hall.

Because Amity is now Bound. And protecting Askala is her responsibility.

Others join her, filling the cramped space, all with the same goal—exiting the maze of corridors that make up the Oasis.

The regular drills to prepare them for such a threat have ensured leaving is an orderly process. No one shoves or jostles. Amity slows down, slipping into line, throwing a quick smile at the Bound behind her. It would almost be military in precision if the people marching up the stairs weren't so conscious of being considerate and courteous. Everyone checks those in front and behind. The person last in the line will ensure everyone reaches their goal.

The bridge.

The warm night air, heavy with pine, envelops Amity as she reaches the outside. She grabs one of the torches left beside the railing so their solar panels can charge during the day, hoping it's a working one. With limited resources, their batteries are slowly dying, but there's no alternative.

Fire is used sparingly in Askala. Especially near a bridge that's largely built of timber to stop it being eaten away by an acidic ocean.

Remnants on the bridge. Amity's breath is huffing, and not from exertion. She's never seen a Remnant—none have come over the bridge since her Proving almost a year ago. Some even wondered if there were any left, lulling Askala into a false sense of security.

But Amity's heard the stories.

Dirty. Desperate. Thinking only of themselves. Some beg, but most try to take by force.

And if one steps foot on land, they're entitled to stay.

Not sure how she feels about that, Amity strikes east along with the others. The foolish assumption that resources are infinite died with the majority of humanity.

Except the belief that everyone deserves a chance is as part of her DNA as her hair color.

As the hulk of the Oasis disappears behind her, Amity realizes that if any Remnants make it, they could be part of this year's Proving. She shakes her head. No Remnant who's made it to Askala has ever passed a Proving. They inevitably become Unbound.

Those the Bound have a responsibility to care for.

The fence surrounding the gardens looms before her, a solid wall of timber designed to keep the dangers of Askala out. Her flashlight strikes over the newly repaired section they just finished working on yesterday. Pale timber waiting to be blackened by storms or carved by claws.

Hopefully this season the plants will survive long enough to produce seeds...

Next is the lab. One of the few relics to survive intact from before the thaw, its round roof crouches low among the pines. Amity shakes her head at the irony. It was built to withstand long winters and heavy snowfall, but the humans who designed it never considered there would come a time when snow didn't exist.

Once known as Alaska, this land was home to frigid winters and landscapes molded by ice.

What's left of it after the rising of the oceans is Askala, a temperate island covered in forests of pine. Snow is a fable that Amity has never seen.

In the end, the lab outlasted an ice age that never arrived. Instead, the pale, squat building survived raging storms that felt like they would never end and forest fires that shouldn't have been possible so far north. Now, it's where the Provings are held.

Once she's past the lab, Amity breaks into a jog. She moves as fast as she can considering the army of pines between the Oasis and the bridge. The other Bounds do the same, spreading out as they head east to the sea. She hangs back, making sure the others are getting through okay. All it takes is one unseen branch and someone could be hurt.

Once everyone passes and melds into the forest safely, Amity prepares to run again, only to freeze when a soft cry comes from her left. Angling her torch, Amity ducks around a handful of trunks to find the source. Nellie, one of the other Bounds, has collapsed on the ground.

"Amity! Thank Terra, my torch cut out and a moment later, my foot was caught." She reaches down, tugging and pulling, but seems to be stuck fast.

Amity shines her light down, revealing Nellie's foot jammed amongst the tangled roots of a mangrove pine.

Nellie's torch flickers back to life. "Of course, now it decides to work."

Amity almost smiles, imagining Nellie's eye roll. "Here, hold this." Passing her the torch, Amity kneels down and grips the roots, yanking and bending them with all her might. The fibrous ropes creak and bend and with a quick tug, Nellie pulls her foot out.

"Thank you, Amity. Not only could I not see my foot to get it free, I'm not sure I would've had the strength to do that so quickly."

Amity smiles at the wafer-thin woman. "That's because of that brood of children you have, running you ragged."

Nellie smiles with pride. She's fulfilled her duty as a Bound well. Straightening, she dusts herself off. "Here." She passes Amity a torch. "Oh, wrong one."

Amity waves the other torch away. "It doesn't matter. We'd better hurry."

Nellie nods and strides away. She turns back when she sees Amity hanging back. "Are you coming?"

Amity smiles. "I'll be right behind you."

Nellie angles her beam of light at the ground, obviously trying to avoid another fall, and dashes off. Amity holds still in the dark, listening for any other sounds of distress. When the forest carries nothing but the sound of voices ahead, she decides it's safe to move forward. It looks like everyone will get there okay.

She's about to break into a run herself, when the light of her torch stutters, like a blinking eye opening and closing. She frowns as she shakes it, then whacks the base on her palm. Everything turns black as the torch dies, forcing her stop.

Ahead of her, beams of light dance through the forest. All she has to do is call out and someone will come. Together, they'll head to the beach.

She pauses, realizing a part of her doesn't want to keep moving ahead. Irrespective of the outcome, what's about to happen to the Remnants will be painful. And when you're raised and groomed and valued to be empathetic, others' pain only compounds your own.

Except she's Bound. Bound to a duty. A responsibility to something far greater than her.

Her mouth opens, ready to call out when one of those beams spins around and strikes her across the face, causing her to raise her arm and shield her eyes.

"Amity?"

She relaxes as she recognizes the voice. A familiar voice, a voice she's known all her life. "Callix. My torch died."

"About half of them have. I thought I'd check to make sure no one got left behind."

Of course Callix would do that. It's what Bounds do.

He scans her with the light, and Amity wishes she could do the same to him. Checking that others are okay is like breathing to her. How is Callix feeling? Is his heart a drum in his chest like hers? Is his mussed blond hair messier than usual, are his strong features tight with tension? Instead, she asks. "What about you? Are you okay?"

"You don't need to worry about me." There's a pause, and Amity wishes she could see why. "Quick. We're going to need everybody there."

Forming a line. Waiting for a choice to be made. Enforcing the consequences of that decision.

5

Amity nods, then realizes her friend can't see it. She swallows. "Yeah, we need to hurry."

Callix grabs her hand, its size and warmth so familiar it's a comfort, and they head through the trees guided by his beam of light.

There were countless days they would run through the forest like this. Laughing as they ducked from one area of dappled shade to the next, thinking the sun's bright rays could never harm them. As they grew older, accepting the flowing hemp robes that protect their skin were necessary, they'd spend hours, tucked tight into roots of a mangrove pine, guessing and wondering what the tests of the Proving might be.

Desperately hoping they'd pass.

Wondering what life would be like if they didn't.

But the day it was announced who would be Bound and who would be left Unbound was a celebration for both of them. Callix had lifted her and spun her around, the decrepit ballroom the ceremony was held in spinning crazily.

They'd passed. They were Bound.

Her father had wiggled his brows as he'd looked at Callix meaningfully. Amity remembers flushing as she'd pulled away. She loves Callix.

As a brother.

Except now she's Bound, she's expected to have children. To pass on her sought-after genes to the next generation.

They're close when Callix abruptly stops. Amity glances around in alarm. Has someone fallen over? She sucks in a breath. Have the Remnants got through already?

Callix turns back to Amity. "Are you okay?"

If Callix didn't know her so well, Amity would've wondered if he could hear the sound of her heart pounding on her ribs. She relaxes a little, touched at her best friend's concern. "I'm okay."

Callix pauses, recognizing the lie for what it is. "Just remember, you're not alone, okay?"

Amity nods. There isn't a Bound who wouldn't lay down their life for another. "What do you think is going to happen?"

Callix looks away. "That will be up to the Remnants."

Amity tightens her hold on his hand. This is going to be hard to watch.

He turns back, his body tight with tension. "No matter what happens, just don't let it get to you, okay?"

Amity doesn't answer. She doesn't know how to do things any other way. She was bred to care.

They all were.

Callix pulls her into a fierce hug. Amity hates the infinitesimal pause before she returns the embrace. She was always so comfortable with Callix. Hugging him was like hugging one of her family. But that was before the Proving.

Before she started to wonder if Callix wanted more.

Before she started to wonder whether she should be wanting more...

They turn and head back through the trees. The scent of the ocean tells Amity they're almost there. Salty, and slightly sulfurous. It's like life and death moving and crashing together, fighting a war where the winner hasn't been decided yet.

The other Bounds are there. Three feet apart, lining the beach. Close enough to be seen, but far enough that the lapping waves can't touch them. Incidental touch of the ocean won't hurt.

But prolonged exposure to the acidic salt water erodes the skin. First it stings, then your eyes burn, then layer after layer starts peeling.

Eventually, it means death, even your bones dissolved by the corrosive water. A few hours, and it's like you never existed.

Shuddering, Amity takes her place. Callix is beside her. She

7

wishes they were close enough to hold hands again. Goose-bumps rise over her skin, despite the warm air.

The High Bound are already on the bridge. They will negotiate with the Remnants.

Her mother is there. Callix's parents at the front, as direct descendants of the man who founded Askala. The one who came up with the solution to the destruction humanity has wreaked.

The sounds of heavy footfall clattering on timber rises over the crash of waves.

They're almost here.

Amity's shoulders straighten. They're a united front. A statement of peace, but one of resistance. We now live in a world where only the deserving survive.

What the Remnants do with that is their choice.

MAGNUS

*D*eciding to join the Bounds on the beach wasn't an easy call, and Magnus is a little surprised to find himself almost there.

Maybe it's because he assumed it would take a little longer to negotiate the forest. All the torches were gone by the time he'd weighed it up. As he'd strode through the forest, he'd realized he didn't need one. In part because he's not trying to run at breakneck speed, but mostly because he knows this forest as well as he knows the maze of the Oasis. In fact, he's spent more time among the mangrove pines than the cramped quarters of the massive, beached cruise ship they call home.

As he sees the line of people along the beach in the dappled moonlight, Magnus's pulse trips through his body. He's not a Bound yet, so technically he shouldn't be here. He's been counting down the hours to his Proving in a few days, when his future will be decided. He's calculated the probability over and over, as if worried the number would change. His whole family are Bounds—his parents are descendants of the first Bound, his brother, Callix, passed his Proving last year. The odds are high he'll join his family. Then he'll be able to find out if he's too late to follow his heart.

But it's not guaranteed.

Knowing that Remnants are approaching had him climbing out of bed. Knowing his whole family was going to be there to meet them had him leaving the ship.

As he'd walked down the gangplank, he'd stopped and wondered whether he should turn around. He's not Bound. He should be back inside, waiting with the Unbounds. He should be showing that following orders is second nature.

In the end, it was one final piece of information that had him striding through the forest.

One person.

Magnus finds her despite the dark, despite the people lining the beach.

It's like she's his center of gravity. The sun he orbits.

Dark hair a thick braid down her back, her hemp clothing tugging at her slim figure in the ocean breeze, Amity stands with her legs slightly apart, her body unmoving as she faces the bridge.

She looks strong. Determined.

But when she tucks a stray strand of hair behind her ear, Magnus knows it's a front. He's spent long enough watching to know that means she's nervous.

Magnus pauses. Wanting to go to her.

But that's not the relationship they have.

At least Callix is beside her, a few feet to the left. His shoulders are pulled back as far they can go, his feet pushed firmly into the sand. He'd be wishing he was up there on the bridge with the High Bound, being part of the negotiations. He's ready to answer the call if the Remnants act without thinking.

Magnus holds back along the tree line. If things go peacefully, he'll meld back into the forest and return to the Oasis before anyone knows he was gone. He'll know his family are okay.

He'll know Amity is safe.

The bridge looms ahead, spearing in the dark unknown. Their final link to the Outlands. No one has ever left Askala by that route—why would they want to? Well, no one has left by choice...

But Remnants come. Magnus doesn't know what they're told about Askala, but he does know that although they're becoming fewer, they're becoming more desperate.

His father is there with the other High Bounds, standing in the shape of an arrowhead with his father at the peak. They're waiting to ask the question.

Clattering sounds of footfalls on the bridge has Magnus tensing, eyes darting to Amity.

They're here.

"Stop!" Magnus's father's voice booms through the dark, deep with authority.

The footsteps halt, and Magnus squints. They're a shadowy mass still a distance away, but it looks like there's about eight of them. He hears Amity's gasp as he realizes about half are women. One of them is a child.

Magnus moves a little closer, the motion almost unconscious, but then stops himself. Amity doesn't need to see them to imagine their fear and their pain. She'd be imagining it so strongly she'd be feeling it alongside them.

This is why Magnus came, even though he's not in a position to help her. It will be hard for Amity to see what's probably going to happen. She knows it's necessary, and why, but that doesn't make it any easier.

A man takes a step forward, breaking away from the others. "Let us through—we mean no harm. We have women and children. We're starving."

11

"The world of plenty was taken from all of us," Magnus's father replies. "Why should we let you pass?"

Magnus mouths the question along with his father. It's the question every group of Remnants is asked. Just like the Proving, it's a test.

Their answer will seal their fate.

"We don't want to fight," says the male voice. He must've been chosen to be their spokesperson. Magnus wonders on what grounds they decided he was the best person to represent them.

His ability to negotiate? Or his ability to fight...

"Neither do we. Answer the question—why should we let you pass?"

Magnus hears the steel in his father's voice, and he silently shifts a little closer to Amity. He knows that hard note. He won't ask the question again.

Tension is winding through the Bounds along the shoreline, taut bodies on high alert. The Remnant's response dictates what will happen next.

"You obviously don't realize where we've come from," the man shouts. "The world beyond the bridge is harsher than you know—if starvation doesn't kill us, disease will. Survival is a game that most don't win. It makes people desperate." There's the slightest of pauses. "It makes people do things they aren't proud of."

The threat in the man's voice is obvious. The older Bounds are already moving forward. They've seen this before and know how it's going to end.

Magnus imagines how his father's lips just thinned, deep in his beard. "Then I'm afraid we cannot let you pass."

A woman in the group cries out, clutching the child to her. Some of the others shuffle closer, most straighten like arrows that have just been notched.

The man takes a step forward. "We didn't think you'd welcome us with open arms."

"Bounds!" Magnus's father's voice booms. "To the bridge!"

Amity's gasp pulls Magnus to her side like a magnet. She spins around, her eyes widening. "Magnus."

Magnus doesn't say anything, finding himself tongue tied like he always is around her. What's he supposed to say? I came here because I had to make sure you're okay? He's not Bound. He's nothing more than her best friend's younger brother. Instead, he turns toward the bridge, pretending this was all that's brought him here.

Callix spins around toward Amity, his brows contracting even tighter when he sees Magnus. "You shouldn't be here."

Magnus doesn't answer. Callix is right, but there's no way he's leaving.

Callix turns back to Amity, probably realizing there's no time to discuss this. "You stay here. They'll need the strongest Bounds to do this."

Amity is already nodding. "I know. You go."

Callix glances at Amity, obviously torn. Magnus grabs his shoulder. "Go, I'll make sure she's okay."

Callix hesitates, but then their father calls for the Bounds again. With a fierce glance directed at Magnus, he heads to the bridge. He'll make sure he's beside their father. More bodies step onto the bridge, heading to meet the Remnants. There's still some distance between them, but the Remnants will move forward any moment.

The tremors coursing through Amity's body are barely there, but Magnus notices. He wonders if his brother did, too. His hand twitches by his side, wishing he could offer her more than just words. "He'll be okay."

"It's more the others I'm worried about," she whispers as she watches the Remnants opening up like a black flower. They're spreading out—will they do the smart thing and retreat?

13

Guilty at the relief that Amity isn't fretting over his brother, Magnus focuses on them, too. He frowns. "They've come here to fight."

They've already sealed their fate.

"Of course they have. They're fighting for their lives."

Which is what Magnus suspected Amity would say. All the Bounds have been selected for their empathy, but Amity seems to feel things more acutely.

Magnus nods. "Yes, what they're doing is understandable. The challenge is to balance one person's pain against that of something so much bigger than us."

She tears her eyes away to look at him, and he freezes. Amity has eyes the color of the earth he loves—a color so much bigger than himself. Each time he gazes into them, he feels like he just speared roots into the soil...as an eagle takes flight in his chest. As with every other time, he looks away. "We're not doing this for us, Amity. We're doing this for Earth."

The Remnants can't come to shore. They think only of themselves.

She doesn't respond, and he's unsure of what that means. He hadn't intended to speak so much.

The ominous drumbeat of footsteps on the bridge has them both looking back toward it. The Bounds have joined the High Bounds, prepared to do what it takes. The Remnants spread out even wider.

Also prepared to do what it takes.

"Magnus!" Amity gasps. "Look!"

A bright orange shape catches the dull moonlight. It's the child, wearing an old life vest of some sort. Magnus peers closer, a little disbelieving. Yes, a life vest. They're almost a relic nowadays, leftover from a time when people chose to frolic in the sea.

Now, the ocean that's swallowed so much of the land is little more than a toxic pool housing any species tough enough to adapt to its acidic waters. A floatation device is just a vest to wear to your funeral.

Someone hoists the child up, a pale beacon on the dark bridge. The woman moves the child to the right, coming closer and closer to the side and Magnus sees that it's a girl. He frowns. A railing lines the entire length of the bridge. Maybe she's trying to get her daughter out of the way, not realizing it won't matter. He wishes Amity didn't have to see this. The pain of these memories will echo long after the Remnants are gone.

"No!" Amity calls out as Magnus watches the orange vest wrapped around a small body being flung into the air. It arches in the midnight sky, hovers as Magnus holds his breath and knows that gravity will do what it does, irrespective of the vulnerable being it holds. The laws of nature cannot be messed with. They're living in a world that's a testament to that.

With a splash, the girl lands in the sea.

Amity rushes to the edge of the water. "She threw her in!"

Magnus joins her, the shock of what just happened morphing to horror. "She thinks she's saving her!"

The girl starts paddling as the waves gently bob her up and down, making her look like a fragile buoy.

Remnants have tried to swim from that point before, but none have made it. The distance, the currents, the water that slowly erodes your skin all take their toll.

"Maybe she'll make it with the life vest," Magnus mutters, not really believing it.

Against the odds, the girl makes small gains toward shore. Maybe the current is in her favor.

"Help me!" The girl's voice is faint but unmistakable.

"She's a child, Magnus." Amity's words are so full of agony that Magnus's heart clenches. She turns to him, eyes wide with fright. "The leatherskins."

Before he can respond that there's been no sign of the

sharks, Amity is gone. Running through the waves, water spraying out wildly, she heads for the girl.

"Amity!"

There are very few shallows off the edge of Askala, there's barely a beach leading to the water. This is the new boundary of an island created by a hungry, rising sea. It means there's a massive ledge that drops deep into the sea, and Amity is about to hit it.

Just as he predicted, Amity's head drops and his heart bottoms out. He runs forward and the warm ocean wraps around his ankles. "Amity. It's not safe!"

The girl is a Remnant, the leftovers of a humanity that created the destruction they're now struggling to survive in. This child's fate was decided when her parents approached Askala with a commitment to violence.

When her mother threw her into the ocean.

But for Amity, none of that matters. A child is hurting. A child could die.

Her lithe body has struck a rhythm slicing through the sea. She's on a direct trajectory to the bobbing girl.

Following Amity is a given. Her presence in his life is as vital as air, even if he can never tell anybody how he feels. Magnus breaks into a run, the water splashing at his shins, then swirling around his thighs.

The body of water slows him down, and frustration fills his muscles. Another step and the ground disappears beneath his feet. He's swallowed by warm water that should feel safe. Instead, his heart thumps hard, as if it's counting the seconds he'll start to feel its effects.

Desperately, he tries to keep his head above the surface. The eyes are the most vulnerable to the corrosive water. But it's unavoidable as the waves come at him, washing over his head. It stings, and Magnus tells himself it's the salt. He can't close his eyes.

He has to get to Amity.

Her black hair is harder to find in the dark ocean, and he only catches glimpses as the water rises and lowers them both. It's all he needs, though. Amity is his target, and nothing will stop him from getting to her.

She's closing in on the child. The little girl, around eight years old, sobs and sputters and she starts to paddle frantically. "Please, help me!"

Amity doesn't respond, staying focused on getting closer. They've all been told that they need to keep their mouths closed if they're unlucky enough to find themselves in the ocean.

Magnus pulls hard through the water, kicking with all his might. He's spent countless hours hiking Askala, meaning he'd be a much stronger swimmer than Amity. Maybe he'll be able to catch up before she gets to the child.

He's just about to risk a mouthful of corrosive saltwater to call out to her when Amity reaches the little girl.

"It's okay, I've got—"

Amity's words are broken off as the girl launches at her, scrabbling desperately. "My vest! It's falling apart!"

Amity goes under as the girl claws at her. Amity's head breaches the water, and her gasp for air spears straight into Magnus's heart. A burst of strength he didn't know he had pulls him through the water to her.

The girl is sobbing, working desperately to keep herself above water. By now, her skin would be stinging and angry red, her eyes streaming. Amity goes under again as Magnus reaches her.

In the same moment he sees the unmistakable fin of a leatherskin weaving toward them.

Adrenalin jolts through his veins so hard he can barely think, but it doesn't matter—he doesn't need to. The drive to save Amity is instinct.

He reaches her just as her head surfaces, the draw for air so much more desperate than the last. But before he can grab her, the gasp is cut off as the child submerges her again.

Diving down, Magnus ignores the sensation of fire slashing over his eyes as he keeps them open. He needs to find Amity before this girl drowns her.

Although the water is nothing but ink, the flurry of bubbles from Amity and the girl's frantic movements let him know where they are. He reaches out, lungs screaming for air as his eyes feel like they're being eroded away, and his heart lurches as he connects with an arm. Hauling up hard, he kicks for the surface.

They all emerge and the girl screams. "The water, it's hurting me! Please! I'm going to drown!"

"Stop moving!" Magnus shouts, about to explain it'll only attract the leatherskin, but the girl's already clambering over Amity as if she's the floatation device she's fast losing. Except Amity sinks, the eyes that were wide with alarm squeezing shut just in time.

Magnus grabs the girl's arms, hoping to pull her off before she drowns Amity. He'll take her to shore himself if it means so much to Amity. The girl shrieks, trying to shove him away, but it's enough for Amity to surface again.

"Magnus," she gasps.

"I've got her." Determination hardens every muscle in Magnus's body and he hauls on the girl. He channels all the anger at this human for endangering Amity purely for her own survival, even though he knows it isn't her fault.

With a huge pull, he drags her to him, disentangling her from Amity, who breaches the surface, gulping for air.

"We need to get back—"

His words freeze in his throat when he sees the leatherskin is coming faster than he realized. Grabbing the girl tightly, he screams. "Amity!"

The fin slicing through the water is two feet high, a mottled

18

gray sail undeniably heading their way. The girl stills, her whimper a mewl of fear.

"Start swimming!" Magnus shouts.

Amity spins around, sees the deadly predator closing in, and turns back. "We have to get her to shore!"

Flipping the girl onto her back, claws through the water. "I've got her. Get moving, Amity!"

Amity swims to his side, grabbing the other side of the girl's life vest. "We'll both do it." One hand grabbing the vest, she strikes out with the other.

Frustration meets a grudging respect as Magnus starts to swim. He should've known Amity would never go ahead without the girl.

As they strike for shore, Magnus knows there's no chance they'll make it. Leatherskins are at the top of the food chain, in part because they're one of the few species tough enough to withstand a heated, acid ocean, but also because they're fast.

And because they're cold-blooded killers.

The girl shrieks, and Magnus and Amity pull through the water even harder. She thrashes, and Magnus yanks hard, grunting at the weight. The shrieks grow to a scream so cold with terror that it freezes his blood. That's not the sound of a girl desperate to stay above water.

A glance over his shoulder tells him why the girl just multiplied in weight.

The leatherskin has latched onto its prey.

The girl's foot is trapped in its unforgiving jaws, and she twists and wails as she desperately tries to free it.

Magnus releases the girl and moves down so he can kick at the beast. His feet hit its tough hide, thudding against the layers of muscle that make up this animal. It makes no difference. The black flecks of eyes stare at him, emotionless and fixated.

The leatherskin opens its mouth again as it surges forward, rows of sharp teeth a garish white in the dark night, then chomps down on the girl's hips with ferocity. Bones crack and flesh tears. Now that it has a solid grip, the shark yanks the girl out of their hands like a doll. The girl's screams are abruptly cut off as she's plunged into the depths of the ocean.

Silence reigns, a glaring contrast to the cries of death that filled Magnus's ears. Breathing heavily, his skin feeling like it's been abraded with sandpaper, he turns to Amity. "You're okay?"

She nods, earth-colored eyes wide and luminous above the water. She glances to where the girl was taken under, and he sees her lip tremble. Knowing she's hurting, but conscious they're far from safe, Magnus swims over. "We need to get out of here."

"But—"

Of course she'd think of the girl before herself.

"No, Amity. There's nothing we can do for her."

As if to prove his point, dark red liquid balloons up from the depths, billowing like sick clouds around them.

Amity jerks back at the sight of the blood, a small cry escaping her. Magnus's heart clenches. He grabs her hand, finding it cold despite the warm water. "Please, Amity."

Bobbing in the water, she stares at him, and for the first time, he holds her gaze. Her life depends on this choice.

"You're right. We need to get to safety."

Relief is a tsunami through his body. Magnus releases her hand almost hastily. All he needed was to make sure she saw reason.

They strike for shore, and although he's the stronger swimmer, he hangs back half a body length. If the leatherskin decides it wants a second course, it's going to have to get through him first.

He sees when Amity tires—her arms barely lift above the water, her legs half-flop, half-kick below the surface.

Magnus pulls up beside her, his eyes feeling raw. "We're

almost there." He indicates the shore not too far away. "You've got this."

Even in the dark, Magnus can see the redness staining Amity's face. She nods, breathing too hard to talk.

When his feet hit solid ground, Magnus's chest loosens. Almost there.

Amity finds the shore a moment later, only to be knocked over by a wave. Magnus jumps forward, dragging her up from beneath the water. She struggles to stand, exhausted from the swim, the near drowning, the toll of the corrosive water, and now the pull of the waves.

Grabbing her around her waist, Magnus hauls her to his side. Waves buffet him from behind, then yank at his legs a moment later, but he ignores it. He ignores everything—the trembling of his tired muscles, the sting of water that should never have become the danger it is, the pull of an ocean that doesn't want them to leave.

He focuses on getting the girl he loves to safety.

It feels like hours, even though it's probably minutes, but Magnus drags Amity out of the water. The moment they're out of its reach, they collapse.

Magnus's breath is a storm in his chest, desperately working to get more air. It swallows all sound, until he realizes he can't hear Amity's.

The rocky soil digs into Magnus's back and arms as he rolls over, leaning above Amity. "Amity!" Frantically, he brushes her dark hair from her face, fear throbbing hard through his veins.

Her eyes flutter open as he registers her lips are parted, her own panting breaths proof she's alive.

Magnus's hand jerks back. He was stroking her face like he had a right to.

Magnus has never touched Amity. In fact, he's avoided it. It was his way of protecting the heart that feels so much for this girl.

21

He knew it would feel like dreams coming true. He knew he wouldn't want to stop.

"Magnus?"

There's something in Amity's voice that has him pausing. There's surprise in there, but he heard that the time a rabbit made its way to the dining hall. There's disbelief, but he heard that when she learned she passed her Proving.

This time, there's a huskiness, a touch of amazement, that he's not even sure Amity has ever heard herself use.

Is it possible she feels it, too?

"Amity." Magnus means to say her name like anyone else would. Her parents. Her friends. The other Bounds.

But he part-whispers it, part-groans it. It's a single word with far too much emotion weighing it down.

Amity blinks in the dark. "You…thank you for saving me."

Voices call from the dark. Some of the other Bounds must've seen them. His time with Amity is over.

He shrugs as he pushes himself up to a sitting position, looking away. "It wasn't a choice."

"They're over here!"

"I…" Amity's voice trails away and Magnus resists the temptation to look back at her. "You'll make a good Bound, Magnus."

That has Magnus spinning around. Does Amity realize what that could mean? She holds his gaze with her earth-colored eyes.

"Sweet Terra, Amity! Are you okay?"

It's Kimina, Amity's mother.

Magnus moves back as Kimina falls to her knees beside her daughter, half-crying, half-shouting at her daughter for making such a rash decision.

Pushing himself to his feet, he waves away the hands that reach for him. "I'm okay. We weren't hurt."

Although, they can't say the same for the little girl.

So much desperation. A mother who threw her child into a

22

deadly sea. A child who was so focused on her own survival, she almost took Amity with her to her death.

Magnus squares his shoulders. They've been told over and over again there's no room for those sort of people in Earth's future.

He glances back, seeing Amity being lifted to her feet.

Amity is safe. That's enough.

For now.

CALLIX

*C*allix twirls his Bound ring around his finger as a sick feeling pools in the pit of his stomach. The sickness climbs up his esophagus and acid burns the back of his throat.

Acid.

Just like the swirling liquid that poor girl had been tossed into when her mother had thrown her from the bridge. Except he can swallow this acid down, whereas that girl had been set to dissolve until the flesh tore from her bones.

But Amity hadn't been able to stand by and let that happen. Her heart is too big, too kind, for her to deafen her ears to a child calling for help.

Callix had watched from the bridge, helpless, as Amity swam to the girl, putting herself at risk without a second thought. And although he'd been distressed, he hadn't been surprised by her actions, fearing that was exactly what she'd do the moment he'd seen the child leave the bridge. Because nobody knows Amity as well as he does. Nobody else has spent as much time by her side.

Everything in him had wanted to jump in and save her, but he'd hesitated, knowing that would go against what it means to be Bound, and that fraction in time had cost him dearly. Just how dearly, he was still trying to figure out. If Magnus had also hesitated...well, it's safe to say that Amity's flesh would be mingling with that girl's in the belly of the shark.

But having watched the girl he loves almost die isn't what's making him feel sick.

It's Magnus.

His younger brother. Smarter than him. Taller than him. Better looking than him. Braver, too. And as if all that isn't bad enough, now Magnus has one other thing on Callix.

He has Amity.

Because there's no mistaking the way she's looking at Magnus as they stand safely on the shore. Her gaze isn't the sort used for her best friend's little brother. It's the same gaze Callix knows he uses when he looks at her. Like Magnus isn't just her past and her future, he's her everything right now.

Tearing his eyes away from his future-stealing brother, Callix positions himself as close to his father on the bridge as possible, keen to prove his worth. *He* didn't break the rules by entering the water. *He* didn't try to haul a Remnant to shore. *He* didn't put the needs of one ahead of the needs of many. Let alone attend a Remnant attack before he'd been made Bound.

But his father doesn't notice him in the chaos. He's called the Bounds to the bridge for a reason. Their drills have prepared them for this moment and they all know what they need to do.

"Trapdoor open!" shouts his father. As the leader of the High Bounds this is his call to make, and now that a child's been thrown from the bridge, it's an easy decision. These Remnants failed their test by demonstrating that they haven't come to Askala in peace. If only they'd known how easy it would have been to pass...

"Trapdoor open!" call the other High Bounds in response, as the Bounds run to the ropes and begin to pull. As one of the strongest of the Bounds, this includes Callix, who takes hold of a rope, his muscles flexing as he grips it.

"Heave!" they call in unison. Callix passes one hand over the other and a hidden section of the bridge splits open like the gaping jaws of a leatherskin. "Heave!"

Realizing what's happening, the Remnants scurry, trying to find a foothold. It's difficult to watch, but Callix reminds himself of the Remnant throwing her child into the deadly water. If that ocean is good enough for a child, it's good enough for all of them.

The Bounds hold steady on the Askala side of the bridge, which has remained solid and Callix continues to haul on the rope. He flinches as the trapdoor drops open with a thud, and the Remnants lose their footing on the bridge, hurtling into the water, screaming from both the pain of their fall and what they know is to come.

There's a reason why there are many ropes attached to the trapdoor, when the job could be done with one. Responsibility for such an action is easier to live with when it's shared. Callix is certainly grateful of that right now. It's hard enough as it is, listening to those screams and knowing the part he's played in causing them.

This world their ancestors created wasn't supposed to be like this. Askala was a sanctuary. A place where both humans and the earth below their feet could heal. But this reality is a little different.

The bridge connecting them to the Outlands has remained as a symbol of welcome and Callix shakes his head at the welcome they just provided. There's been talk among the Bounds of burning the bridge to protect Askala. Talk that's been putting light behind Magnus's eyes while robbing Callix of his ability to speak. He can't bring himself to tell his father he disagrees. The Bounds are meant to follow. The High Bounds are meant to lead.

Callix winces as he lets the rope fall and he inspects the blister that's burnt into the palm of his hand. His first thought is that he'll ask Amity to rub a balm into it, his second is now he'll have to do it himself.

The screaming of the Remnants is weakening with each life that's lost, replaced by an eerie silence echoing across the water. Is this what kindness look like? But then again, letting these invaders come ashore would have put even more lives at risk. It could have jeopardized not only the future of the human species, but the entire planet. It seems kindness can be judged in more ways than one.

"Good job, Bounds!" Callix's father punches his fist in the air and the silence is filled with cheers. The Remnants' demise is Askala's victory.

Callix's father opens his fist and turns his palm to the Bounds who respond by raising their left hands, their Bound rings a silver streak across their fourth finger, a symbol of what binds them to the Earth.

Scanning the shoreline for Amity, Callix catches sight of Magnus, a painfully familiar long dark braid bobbing beside him. They disappear into the chaos of Bounds and Callix cranes his neck, unable to find them again. The look on the faces of the Bounds shows they're torn between their relief of not having to make way for the Remnants and their devastation at having to watch them suffer and die.

It's easier when the Remnants die away from their eyes. When they perish in their own homes or are swept away by the relentless tornadoes. When they can pretend there's nothing they can do for them, when the truth is that they could have saved every last one of those Remnants on the bridge... at the expense of the greater good. Which isn't something any of them are willing to do, including Callix. They'd failed to come in peace. They could never have been welcomed.

The greater good. They have a system here and it works. A

system that ensures the survival of both the planet and the human race by guaranteeing that nothing like the catastrophes Earth has suffered will ever happen again. If the Remnants are allowed to tear that system down then their fragile planet will wither and die, taking all of them with it.

As the cries from the last Remnant are swallowed by the ocean, the Bounds leave the bridge. Their job here is done. The trapdoor will remain open for seven days, long enough to eliminate possible survival of any Remnants waiting on the other side. Long enough, also, for the Bounds to recover from what they'd just witnessed.

Streaming back toward the Oasis now, the Bounds are keen for sleep. Callix knows he'll never sleep again. Well, not properly, anyway. Not with the risk of dreaming of Amity looking at Magnus with eyes that are supposed to be for him. Although, something tells him that this nightmare is about to become one he's going to have while he's awake.

Amity knew she was meant to be with Callix. What else could she have thought when they'd passed their Proving together? She'd hugged him so tightly at their ceremony when they discovered they'd both been made Bound. Although, now that he thought about it, she'd been the one to break away first. And he'd stood there grinning like an idiot, not realizing that the future he'd been tested for might be one devoid of the girl he loves.

His only hope is if Magnus somehow fails his upcoming Proving, something as likely as his father sealing the trapdoor so that Remnants can come and go as they please.

No, Magnus will pass his Proving. He'll probably get the best score Askala has ever seen. Because Magnus is Magnus and everything always goes his way.

"You can head on back now," says Tory, a Bound who passed his Proving several years ahead of Callix. "I'm on watch tonight." Tory lets out a yawn and rubs at his eyes.

28

"I'll do it." Callix pulls back his shoulders and offers Tory a smile. "I need the distraction."

"That was hard to watch, wasn't it?" Tory shakes his head and looks toward the sea.

"It was," says Callix, the Remnants not the first thing to come to mind. "I don't mind watching the bridge for you. I won't sleep anyway. Get back to Nellie and make some more little future Bounds to run riot."

Tory laughs, one foot moving forward, betraying his temptation to accept Callix's offer.

Callix reaches out and takes the ancient bull horn from Tory's hands. The horn is used to alert the Bounds of danger. Its high pitched blast can be heard for miles, the warning then relayed over the speakers in the Oasis, sending people spilling from their beds.

"Go on," says Callix.

"Geez, do they test for bossiness now in the Proving?" laughs Tory. "Because I reckon you'd have the top score."

Callix grins and takes up position at the end of the bridge.

"Sleep tight," he says to Tory's retreating steps.

At last, silence envelopes the air once more. No more screaming. No more heaving. No more younger brothers stealing futures. It's just Callix standing on the end of a bridge that stretches halfway to nowhere.

He draws in a deep breath, trying to still the churning in his gut. He may have been able to delay going back to the Oasis for one night, but he can't delay it forever. Soon, he'll need to return and face the ramifications of what he saw. Face his brother with his handsome face. Face his best friend with her eyes the color of the earth after its been kissed by the rain.

The Oasis will soon be humming with life, the Bounds reminding the Unbounds how lucky they are, reassuring them that their future is safe.

A clunking noise catches Callix's attention and he takes a step down the bridge, tilting his head as he listens.

Nothing. Just the trapdoor banging on the posts of the bridge.

It's easy to get spooked out here. Everyone's been on edge since the disappearance of two Bounds last year who went out to the gardens to dig up carrots and were never seen again. If you could vanish from the face of the Earth doing an innocent task like that, when could you ever feel safe? Certainly, not now.

Clunk.

Callix's heart picks up a beat as he grips the horn tightly and runs down the bridge, pleased he didn't hesitate to react this time. That was no ordinary *clunk.*

Should he sound the horn? He's never actually had to use it before and hadn't expected to when he'd offered to take over from Tory. He'd wanted to be left out here with nothing but his thoughts. He doesn't need an unidentifiable *clunk* for company.

Reaching the trapdoor, he stops and scans for the source of the noise.

Clunk.

Looking down at the severed end of the bridge, he sees a hand. It grips the timber and holds on. Then another hand joins it as a man tries to hoist himself up.

Fighting the urge to stomp on his hands, Callix jumps back, the horn held to his lips but breath failing to leave his lungs. Protocol would have him stop this Remnant. It's his duty to the future of Askala. But... it's one thing to pull on a rope and watch a Remnant fall. It's another to crush a Remnant's fingers underneath his heel and send them screaming to their death. Bounds are chosen for their kindness. Surely asking a Bound to guard the bridge isn't such a smart idea? Because as much as duty is binding him to raise his boot in the air, his heart is preventing him from doing it.

Damn it! He's hesitating again!

Tucking the horn into his pocket, Callix kneels down and reaches out his shaking hand.

"Let me help you," he says. This may not be the right decision, but at least he's managed to make one.

The Remnant grips onto him. The man isn't much older than Callix himself. Wild hair and eyes, his skin red and angry, but still managing to hold onto his bones.

Callix hauls him up to safety, panting with the effort. And now they're face to face. Remnant versus Bound. Old enemies. New friends.

"Are you okay?" asks Callix.

Blinding pain explodes behind Callix's eyes as the Remnant lands a blow on his nose and he hears the cartilage break, shocking him back into the reality of the situation.

This man isn't his friend. He's a Remnant and it's Callix's job to stop him reaching the shoreline or he'll become one of them.

Callix reaches out to grab the Remnant by the shoulders, planting his feet on the rough timber of the bridge so he can shove him back into the water. But the Remnant ducks, stepping aside with ease. Callix is stronger, but this man has clearly had more experience with combat in the Outlands than Callix has had in his gentle life in Askala.

The Remnant reaches behind his back and now he has a weapon balancing in his hands. Callix squints, unable to identify it in the moonlight.

"Out of my way," says the Remnant. "Or you can join my friends for a swim."

With blood now pouring from his nose, and his head feeling like it might float up to the stars, Callix steps back. He's no match for this Remnant. Once again, his hesitation has cost him. This time, it's cost everyone in Askala. Because his father had made the right call. These Remnants hadn't come in peace. Now they have one more mouth to feed when they can barely feed themselves. And feeding the mouths of men who are dangerous never turns out well. The entire colony is at risk.

The Remnant runs down the bridge and Callix pulls the horn from his pocket and holds it to his mouth. His father is going to be so disappointed in him. But before he can form a seal with his lips, a shadow darts down the bridge toward the Remnant.

The Remnant sees what Callix sees, and fires his weapon, sending flames shooting down the bridge toward the shadow. Callix gasps. A flamethrower! He's never seen one of these before but has heard they're a weapon favored by Remnants, with gas easier to come by than bullets.

But the shadow is fast and dodges the flame, slamming itself into the Remnant and knocking him down, sending the flamethrower scuttling across the bridge.

"Tory!" calls Callix, certain that's who it must be.

"Callix!" the shadow calls in a voice that isn't Tory's, just as a cloud clears the moon, sending light pouring down from the sky.

And Callix sees the face of his savior.

It's Magnus. Of course it's Magnus. It's *always* Magnus.

"Get the weapon!" his brother calls.

Callix launches forward and picks up the flamethrower, just as Magnus lifts the Remnant to his feet and shoves him over the edge of the bridge, his screams swallowed by the darkness below.

"Are you okay?" Magnus runs to Callix, his eyes wide with shock at the sight of him.

Callix nods, trying to bring forward a thank you, but finding it bubbling in the back of his throat, mingling with the blood of his defeat.

Isn't it enough that Magnus has stolen his future? Did he have to take his dignity too? Rescuing him like he's a helpless child.

"Lucky I came back to find you," says Magnus. "That Remnant nearly got to shore."

"I know." Callix swallows down the blood, not needing a reminder of who Magnus has become — the man who doesn't hesitate.

The man who does all the things that somehow Callix fails to do.

MERCY

*M*ercy lags behind the other Bounds on her way back to the hulk of metal that's the Oasis, fighting the temptation to turn back and see why Callix has lingered at the bridge. He wouldn't want her checking on him. He barely knows she exists. She, on the other hand, has been acutely aware of his existence ever since their Proving last year.

She knows he likes to wear his shirt with the top two buttons undone. She knows he sometimes carries books around, but never reads them. She knows his left eye twitches whenever anyone calls him Cal.

She also knows how he looks at Amity. Like she's the only person who matters. She's the reason he never stops to see what else is out there. *Who* else. But when the day comes that he finally opens his eyes, she wants to be there. Right there. The first person he sees.

Because Amity doesn't love him. Not in the way he wants her to. He's been wearing a blindfold his whole life.

He's not the only one who looks at Amity like that, though. She's seen the way Magnus looks at her whenever he lifts his eyes from one of the books he carries and actually reads. Mercy notices things like that, even if nobody else seems to. Maybe that's because nobody else has to study the Bounds in the same way she does.

But she saw Callix on the bridge tonight. Looking at Amity. At *them*. His blindfold was finally lifted, which means that soon his eyes will be ready to see.

She sighs as she returns her torch to the railing and walks up the gangplank of the Oasis, reminding herself that it doesn't matter if Callix ever notices her. They may both be Bound, but they can never be together.

It's this thought that has her deciding not to go directly to her empty cabin in the Oasis where the walls press in on her, crushing her with her loneliness. She considers going to her parents' cabin, but dismisses this idea quickly, not being able to stand the look of pride they've had plastered to their faces ever since she passed her Proving. If only she deserved their pride.

She heads toward the stairwell that will take her to the pool deck. Ronan will be there. And more than she needs anything right now, she needs to be with someone who knows her— really knows her—and loves her anyway.

There's a distinctive smell about the Oasis—stale air laced with rusting metal—and she breathes it in, wondering what this old ship smelled like before a tornado picked it up and slammed it onto dry land. It's hard to imagine it swarming with wealthy passengers stuffing their bellies with food as they danced their way across the dying planet. These days, the ballroom is used for the Provings and the dining halls are filled with both the Bound and Unbound, with stomachs that leave almost as empty as they arrive.

Mercy enters the stairwell, trailing her hand across the cracked plastic sign that points to the pool deck, her bare feet padding on what's left of the frayed carpet.

She takes the stairs two at a time and scans her hand on the sensor at the top landing. Bounds have access to every part of Askala. Nowhere is off limits for these chosen few.

Catching her reflection in the glass panel as the door swings open, she runs a hand through her limp hair. It's no wonder Callix has never noticed her. Plain brown hair, plain brown eyes, plain pale skin and a plain ordinary straight nose. Plain. Unlike Amity with her annoyingly distinct lack of plainness.

She breathes in the fresh night air as she steps out onto the deck, pleased to be outside once more. The stars are bright tonight, reminding her of the fragility of planet Earth. Just one celestial body in a giant cosmos, of no consequence to the universe if it thrives or fails. Humans are doing their best regardless. Even if most of the time it feels too late.

Ronan is standing by what used to be a pool for the wealthy people to swim in when they tired of dancing. Now, it's more of a tank than a pool. Because these days survival trumps entertainment. And humans need pteropods, which in turn, need a tank to breed.

Ronan looks up to see Mercy and breaks into a wide smile, the same sort Callix uses for Amity. His red hair glints in the moonlight and he pulls back his broad shoulders. For a moment she thinks he's going to strut like one of the ravens that nest under the bridge. Her plainness fades away when she looks into his eyes. She's not sure how he does it, but somehow he makes her feel beautiful.

"Thought I'd find you here." She joins him by the tank, peering into the murky depths. "I didn't see you at the bridge."

"Someone had to stay with the pods." He loops his arm around her and she steps closer to rest her head on his chest, listening as his heart rate picks up. He may not be the guy she wants him to be, but right in this moment, he's enough.

"It was awful out there." She lifts her head to look at him in the dim light. "Watching the Remnants die like that wasn't easy. They had a child with them."

"Did any of them make it across?" He skims his fingertips over her hair and she shivers, unsure if it's from the cold or the human contact.

"No." She crouches down at the edge of the pool, an excuse to break away from Ronan and the conflicting feelings he awakens in her. Out here it's easy to fool herself that one day she could love him. Except, she knows she doesn't trust him. She possibly doesn't even like him. But he'd do anything for her and that knowledge never fails to reel her in.

She studies the shadows in the tank, watching as the pteropods swim underneath the layer of phytoplankton that floats on top like a blanket.

Known as the butterflies of the ocean, they're small creatures with glistening wings that glide through the water and an iridescent core that glows through their gelatinous bodies. It's their core that they're bred for. The most precious commodity Askala has to offer.

"Do you want one?" Ronan reaches for a net with a long pole and pokes it into the water.

"But we're not allowed." Mercy looks up at him, her breath catching in her throat. "It's not fair if we have more than our ration. It's for the greater good."

"Screw the greater good." He prods about in the water and a sick feeling weaves its way through her gut. "It could be ages until we get another chance like this."

She swallows and pulls herself to a stand. Normally, a Bound as young as Ronan wouldn't be left alone with something as important as the pteropods. A Remnant invasion is about the only exception, with as many Bounds as possible needed on the shoreline. As Ronan said, someone has to stay behind.

There's a reason for all these rules though, and what Ronan's doing now is exactly it. Bounds shouldn't take more than their share. A herd can't thrive if each man works for himself.

Ronan pulls up the net and squints inside. From where Mercy stands, she counts five pteropods.

"Bingo!" He thrusts the net in her direction and she jumps back as she's sprayed with cool water. "Take one."

"I can't," she says, fully aware that a true Bound wouldn't dream of doing this. Not ever. "It isn't right."

"Who's gonna know?" He holds the net steady and waits.

Reaching out a shaking hand, she's ashamed at how much she wants to take one. He's right. Nobody would know. And it's just one pod. There must be thousands in that tank.

"Quick, before it's too late." He jostles the net at her and before she knows what she's doing, she's grabbed one of the fattest pteropods and stuffed it into her mouth.

Biting down, she winces as the squishy outer layer explodes inside her mouth, releasing a rush of bitter liquid. Closing her eyes, she concentrates on the intensity of the flavor, certain she can already feel the nutrients flowing into her depleted body. Humans could survive on pods alone, if only they had enough.

Ronan scoops up the remaining four pteropods, tossing one into his mouth as he returns the net to its position at the side of the pool.

"Have another." He holds out his open palm and the pods squirm and glow in the warm night air.

Powerless to stop herself, she takes another one, further proof she doesn't deserve to have retained her right to breed. A Bound is normally only rationed one pod per week, which means this week she'll have had triple what any other Bound has had. Apart from Ronan, who's just put the other two in his mouth, taking his count to four... that she knows of.

"This is just like old times." His words are distorted by the pods rolling about on his tongue, but Mercy understands his meaning and it almost stops her heart.

"You said we'd never speak about that again." She wipes her mouth with the back of her hand. Coming up here was a mistake. She doesn't need a reminder of the last time he encouraged her to break the rules. She already thinks of it every minute of every day, wondering if she made the right choice.

"Relax!" He laughs as he taps the side of his nose with his index finger. "Our little secret."

She's not certain this is who she'd choose to be the keeper of her secrets, but she's stuck with him nonetheless.

"Anyway," he says. "I have it on good authority that we're about to have a bumper crop of pteropods. There'll be plenty for everyone. Maybe even enough for double rations. Perhaps the Unbound will be able to have some without having to earn them."

Mercy lets out a slow breath. She's seen this smug look on his face before. He should never have been left alone out here. "Ronan, what have you done?"

"Only what should've been done years ago." He taps his nose again. "These Bounds think they're so smart—"

"Ronan!" She steps up to him and pokes a finger into his chest. "Enough! You can't talk like that. You're a Bound now. We both are. It's not us and them. We *are* them."

"You're right." He takes her finger and pulls her hand to his mouth, brushing his lips across her knuckles, before kissing the back of her hand where the chip lies underneath her skin. "We are Bound."

She pulls her hand away, knowing what comes next. The Bound have a responsibility to breed. Ronan expects she'll choose him. She knows if she doesn't, then he'll tell.

This is why it doesn't matter if Callix sees her. Her future is with Ronan, whether she wants it to be or not.

"Soon," she tells him, knowing she won't be able to put him off much longer.

"How soon?"

The door swings open, saving Mercy from answering the question she wishes he'd never asked. It's Kimina, the High

Bound responsible for the pteropod tank. She's also Amity's mother, which means she's one of the last people Mercy wants to see right now.

"Thanks for holding the fort, Ronan." She strides over to them. "Hello, Mercy."

Mercy blinks twice, surprised she knows her name. "Is Amity okay? I saw what happened out there."

"She's fine." Kimina pulls her lips into a smile that says she doesn't want to talk about this. It's no wonder. Her daughter broke a lot of rules out there tonight.

Ronan shoots Mercy a look, clearly not understanding and Mercy shakes her head. This is a conversation for later.

Kimina paces the length of the tank, her nose twitching, almost as if she can smell the missing pods. And whatever else it is that Ronan's done. "Everything okay here?"

"Never better." Ronan turns his head so he can wink at Mercy without Kimina seeing.

Mercy blanches, knowing for certain now that Ronan's been up to something more than just stealing pods. She knows it by his arrogance. And now she's implicated by association.

"I need to get back to my cabin." Mercy turns on her heels and walks away as quickly as she can without appearing to be rushed.

Pulling open the door, she practically flies down the stairs, desperate for quiet. Reaching the bottom level where all the Bound live, she makes her way through the maze of corridors.

Two more turns and she's in front of her door, waving her hand over the sensor. The door opens and she rushes in and throws herself on her bed, only to find that she was right... the walls are pressing in on her. Only instead of them suffocating her, the isolation feels like a welcome relief.

Perhaps she'd have been better off living the life she was born for.

Unbound.

AMITY

*T*he world is still blurry the following day as Amity navigates her way through the Oasis. Brushing her hand over the walls as she goes, fingers bumping over the peeling paint, she blinks rapidly, trying to bring the world into focus. Her mother said it would take a couple of days for the stinging to subside…after repeatedly pointing out what a stupid decision Amity had made. Between the leatherskin and the toxic water, she's lucky to be here.

At least the redness has gone, the physical reminder of everything that happened yesterday. But the memories, the emotions, have clung to her consciousness like rust.

The little girl, trying so hard to survive. She could feel her misery and pain. Amity shudders as she reaches the stairs. Her mother must've been pretty desperate to do something like throw her child into the ocean and the dangers it holds.

Her hands brush over her belly. She'll be expected to have children soon. It's what Bounds do, their responsibility. If you're given the gift of being chosen to breed, then breed is what you must do.

Would she do the same for her own child if faced with the same choice?

The answer is instantaneous—yes.

She would give her child any chance at survival she could.

Thinking of something so entrenched in her future has her mind turning to the one thing she's avoided.

The one who saved her.

The one whose touch had her discovering new feelings even she, the girl who's experienced a kaleidoscope of emotions in her seventeen years, had never experienced.

Magnus.

How could her response to him be so swift and sharp? It's a question she needs an answer to.

Outside, the sun is high and harsh. Amity wraps her veil around her head, welcoming the shadowy coolness. To think that her Inuit ancestors who were already here before the Oasis was thrown like debris onto their shores, used to wear coats of fur.

But that was before…

Before the fires.

Before the storms.

Before the loss of so many sentient lives it hurts Amity to even think of it.

She shakes her head as she angles for the forest. All that matters now is their responsibility to ensure Earth is never desecrated like that again.

The shadows of the trees quickly envelop her and Amity allows her veil to slip back. She can see why Magnus spends so much time out here. It's a far cry from the cramped, stale conditions of the Oasis.

It's just that the outdoors can almost be as dangerous as the ocean.

Deciding to enjoy the peaceful weather while it lasts, Amity heads north. The terrain hikes up and quickly becomes rough. These elevated areas are all that could keep above the climbing sea levels. Sometimes she imagines the continents as drowning humans, working desperately at keeping their heads above water. Some have little more than their noses staying dry.

As Amity continues to hike through the mangrove pines, she realizes she doesn't really know where Magnus could be. He's such a recluse, that no one raises a brow when he heads for the forest each day, his books in tow.

Which is fine, until you want to find him.

Focusing on the ground, she looks for a track, but there are no obvious trampled paths. That suggests he takes a different route each time, or heads to a different destination. Hoping it's not the second, she looks up at the towering pines, doing some calculations.

Magnus wouldn't go far. Everyone knows it's too dangerous. Her mind scans the mental map she holds of Askala. Magnus loves quiet, and Magnus loves nature.

Tapping into those emotions, Amity closes her eyes. Where would someone feeling like that go?

The lake!

Well, more of a dam really, but it's been optimistically called a lake. A protected body of water that the colony treats so they can use it as drinking water, it's only a few minutes' walk. It's also where a lot of the wildlife can be found.

She heads north, glad it's not far. At least if she's wrong, it won't take much to retrace her steps.

Amity finds him almost straight away, a small bolt of pleasure that she guessed right spearing through her. Magnus's head is down, lost in the pages of the words he's reading, as he sits on a rock. She pauses, taking in the sight. She's pretty sure everyone does that when they first see Magnus.

Amity noticed his good looks long ago, like any other girl on the Oasis had, and not just because Magnus is a direct descendant of the founder of Askala. So is Callix, but even his strong blond features never garnered the same sort of attention.

No, Magnus was molded by the gods of beauty. Dark hair falling over dark, soulful eyes, strong brows that speak of quiet determination, a straight jaw that developed stubble so much earlier than the others.

And in a world where Bound women outnumber Bound men two to one, a handsome male carrying strong Bound genes gets noticed.

Amity was just like the other girls—taking sideways glances in the dining hall, wondering what was percolating behind his thoughtful intensity. But he was so absorbed in his books that she figured there wasn't any point. He barely glanced at her, or anyone else for that matter.

Plus, everyone assumed her friendship with Callix would grow to something more.

That was, until last night.

When Magnus had looked at her, something in his gaze had taken her breath away. Then the way he'd said her name had her heart doing strange acrobatics it's never done before.

It's what has her standing here now. She needs to know—how much of that feeling was her emotion, and how much of it was Magnus's?

As she takes a step, a pebble crunches beneath her shoe and Amity freezes.

Magnus looks up, shock striking across his handsome features before he quickly looks away. "I, ah, didn't hear you." He clears his throat. "Hey, Amity."

Amity smiles as she resumes her approach, ignoring the flutter in her chest like a hundred pteropods are crazy swimming in there. "Whatever you were reading must've been engrossing."

Magnus closes the book, its swollen, warped pages another victim of their broken world. "I, ah, wasn't really reading."

44

Amity glances at the cover. *The Complete Collection of North American Birds.* "I can see why. Nothing more depressing than that."

Magnus glances down, almost looking surprised at what's in his hands. "I like to remind myself."

"Of everything we've lost?"

"Of everything we have a responsibility to repair."

Amity glances at the calm body of water beside them, the trees around them. "That's what you read when you're out here?"

Magnus doesn't answer straight away, and Amity glances at him. He's staring out over the lake, and it strikes her that he's barely made eye contact. Something frowns inside her, unsure what that means.

"Mostly," he shrugs.

Silence slips between them and this time the frown gains body. This almost feels…awkward.

Amity glances at Magnus again, once again trying to decipher how much of this emotion is hers and how much is his.

The issue with being so strong on the empathy front is it's hard to sense another's emotions without them blending with your own. Some days, she feels like a walking sponge.

Magnus picks up a pebble from between his feet, rolling it between his fingers. "Why are you here, Amity?"

At first, Amity figures he's subtly asking her to leave, but then she registers the huskiness in his tone. There's something in the way Magnus says her name…

"I wanted to thank you. For last night. You saved my life."

The fiddling pauses for a split second. "It's what any of us would do for each other."

Which is true. "But you didn't try to stop me, Magnus. And when we needed to return, you let me make the choice."

Some others would've stopped her from getting to the child or they would've demanded they return the moment the leatherskin took her. Magnus told her, but waited for her to decide. What would he have done if she'd said she wanted to stay and look for the girl, despite the deadly shark?

Why does she get the sense that he would've stayed right there with her?

Magnus stills. "My Proving is tomorrow."

Noting the change of topic, Amity doesn't push it. For some reason, Magnus's evasion almost has her smiling. "I know. Pretty nerve-wracking, huh?"

"A lot is riding on it, yes."

Amity's not surprised at the heaviness in his tone. His whole future depends on the Proving. "You'd have to be pretty confident."

Magnus's entire family are Bounds, not only that, his parents are High Bound—two of the ten Bounds who scored the highest on the measures of IQ and emotional intelligence. It's practically guaranteed he'll join them.

"There's always a chance I won't pass."

Amity thinks of her own Proving. Seven days. Three intensive tests where the right answers are so nebulous you have no idea whether you passed until your Announcement ceremony.

Tests that will decide whether you will become Bound, or Unbound…whether you'll have the opportunity to pass on your genes to another generation.

The tests that will dictate whether these feelings she's discovered will even have a chance.

Because if Magnus doesn't pass, then it won't matter. Whatever she's hoping has been sparked would never gain life.

She shakes her head. Of course Magnus will pass.

Although, all it takes is a choice, one that seems right, but is wrong.

She straightens. She shouldn't have come. Until Magnus passes his Proving, all these fledgling feelings have to stay that way. Something bigger than them will decide whether they take flight.

In all honesty, maybe she imagined the chemistry between them last night.

Amity places her hands on the rocks, preparing to push herself up. She'll go see her mother, maybe help out at the pod tank. Right now, she needs to keep busy.

"Look!"

Magnus's voice is barely a whisper, making Amity still as her pulse gallops ahead.

Is it one of the massive mottled grizzlies they share the island with? She was so caught up in her thoughts and emotions she totally forgot to pay attention to her surroundings.

In this world, that error can be fatal.

Magnus leans toward her, pointing up to the sky.

The lone cry of an eagle has her focusing on the circle of blue created by the crowns of the trees. The sleek brown bird, smaller than the ones described in the book Magnus had been holding, is circling the lake.

"Oh." Amity breathes. "It's beautiful."

"They're rare, that's for sure." Magnus's voice is full of the awe that's flowing through Amity. "It's probably come for a drink."

The eagle circles again, tilting its wings with unconscious skill. Amity leans closer to Magnus, trying to get a better look. Another cry echoes through the air—sad and stirring, but somehow laced with warning. Another turn and it lands high in a pine tree, sharp eye angling toward them.

Amity almost smiles. It's not impressed to find them here.

Magnus turns toward her. "We'd better go—"

His words die as he finds her face inches from his.

Amity is instantly captivated by his dark, soul-deep eyes. Memories swirl through her.

Magnus's hand finding hers in the water.

47

Magnus brushing wet hair from her face, voice full of panic.
Surely all of those emotions weren't just hers.

Surely everything she's feeling now can't come from one heart.

Magnus doesn't move, doesn't blink. His gaze absorbs her, studies her. Like a caress over her skin, his intensity grazes over her eyes, her cheeks...her lips.

Warmth like she's never felt before blooms deep in her belly. It spreads up, somehow languid yet an overwhelming rush all at once. It takes her breath away.

It's only when she registers that Magnus hasn't moved away, hasn't taken a breath himself, that she gets her answer.

"This isn't just me, is it, Magnus?"

Magnus pauses, then looks away. "No, Amity. What I feel for you was born a long time ago."

She startles. He's had these feeling longer than she's realized?

He turns back, face stripped naked by the truth. "But unless I'm Bound, none of that matters."

Magnus pushes to his feet, holding out his hand to help Amity up. She glances at it, knowing the motion was probably instinctual. Callix stopped those gentlemanly gestures long ago, knowing Amity would just get up on her own.

But the temptation to touch Magnus again overrides her independent streak. Breath held, she slips her hand into his, revelling in the way Magnus's eyes widen. Bracing herself, she pulls herself up only to find Magnus doing most of the work. With one smooth motion, Amity is standing.

The moment she's upright before him, Magnus releases her hand and turns away. Coolness flows around her body, making Amity realize how warm she just got. Magnus takes a few steps away, visibly pulling in a breath.

Amity hides her smile. Magnus avoiding her over the past couple of years is taking on a whole new light.

The moment she's beside him, Magnus starts to walk,

heading back to the Oasis. Still working on holding in her smile, she falls into step.

Now, the eagle can get its much-needed drink.

Now, Amity can soak up the knowledge that she's not only not alone in these feelings, that it seems Magnus had them long before her. The gentle sounds of the forest climb up around them, although Amity doesn't mind the quiet. It's probably something she'll become familiar with if she starts spending more time with Magnus.

Magnus clears his throat. "Did you know the ants protect the mangrove pines?"

Amity raises her brows, more so because she didn't expect much more conversation. "No, I didn't."

Magnus stays focused on weaving their way through the forest. "Yeah, the ants live among the twisted roots, and depend on the sap produced by them for food. In exchange, the ants chase away the insects that may harm the pines and kill the climbing vines that might choke them."

Amity glances at the pines marching past them. "Huh. That's pretty cool."

As they walk, Magnus talks to her about the intricacy of the ecosystem they're walking through. She knows he's doing it to fill the silence so it doesn't become awkward, but he doesn't realize how much of himself he's revealing.

He's showing how intimately he knows Askala, his tone giving her a glimpse into the reverence he feels for this island. Magnus has never spoken to her this much, and she's discovering how tightly his heart is woven with their home. With Mother Nature.

It tells her that just in the same way he saved her—with gentle determination—he'd do the same for Askala.

They reach the decaying hulk of the cruise ship too soon and Amity realizes she could spend hours like this with Magnus.

They reach the stairwell that will see them go separate ways.

Magnus looks away, and Amity finds herself a little disappointed that they've already defaulted to the way things were. Deciding that going to the pteropod pool is definitely a good idea considering the maelstrom of feelings alive within her right now, she takes the first step to head to the upper deck.

"Amity."

Stopping at the huskiness in his voice, Amity turns. Magnus hasn't moved, not only that, he's staring at her in a way that has her breath hitching.

Magnus swallows, his eyes seeming to be filled with the same storm that's raging inside her. "I'll see you after my Proving."

Amity's hand is holding onto the rail so hard she doesn't know how the decrepit thing doesn't snap. She's not sure if she's stopping herself from running to Magnus, or from running away.

Magnus, beautiful, smart, sensitive Magnus who seems to be just as caught up in this emotional turmoil, is telling her their future depends on those three tests.

If he's Bound—

No. She refuses to let that thought gain momentum.

When he's Bound, then running to him will be a given.

Wishing she could say more, Amity nods. "I'll be there."

Magnus lets out a breath, something bright flashing through his eyes, before he heads down the corridor.

For some reason, that glimmer of light has Amity smiling as she heads up the stairs. Magnus wants her there, waiting. The thought has warmth blossoming through her chest.

The smile is still there when she reaches the upper deck. The pteropod pool sits in the center, a rectangular hole that holds the tiny animals keeping Askala alive.

Amity is just wondering if her lips are going to be angled up all day thanks to the hopeful sun that was just born in her chest when she sees her mother.

And the smile dies.

Kimina is squatting beside the pteropod pool, her brows pulled low in a frown. It's a look she doesn't see often on her mother, the woman who embodies their Inuit heritage. Their ancestors lived through the changes that saw Alaska die and Askala born. The winters that never came, the ravaging storms, the creeping pine forests bringing animals they'd never seen before.

But instead of spawning hopelessness and hatred, Kimina, along with many of the Inuit, had adapted and evolved. They'd learned to find joy in a world where joy was shadowed by survival. It was inevitable they'd become Bounds.

But her mother, the woman who can smile against the odds, is definitely not smiling.

Amity stops beside her. "What's up?"

Kimina points to the water. "Look."

Amity squats too, staring into the pool. Islands of phytoplankton float across the surface, but it's what's underneath that has her focus.

Although they're called butterflies of the ocean, Amity thinks of them as more like fireflies of the deep. They're like orbs of light with wings. Normally, they glide above and below each other, a gentle, constant movement.

But today, they're...slower. Seeming to sit closer to the surface.

Amity frowns, discovering why her mother has lost her peace. "What's wrong with them?"

Kimina stands. "I don't know. Temperature is constant, so is pH."

"Nitrite levels?" If they're too high, it reduces the pteropods' ability to hold oxygen in their body. That would explain the sluggish movement and the surface dwelling.

"A little high, but nothing unusual. I'm going to check iron levels next."

Iron levels. That makes sense. Both phytoplankton and pteropods need the trace element to thrive. It doesn't take much for it to drop and would certainly slow down the pteropods. Most of the colony knows what it feels like to be deficient in nutrients.

Amity stands, although her gaze remains on the pods. What would happen if they lost some?

A gust of wind snaps her out of her worried thoughts.

Kimina brushes a strand of the black hair Amity inherited from her face. She points to the horizon. "We'd better get inside."

Her mother is right. Storm clouds are gathering fast. That's the reality of their world—harsh heat one hour, a raging monsoon the next. All on an island that was never supposed to be part of a temperate climate.

Following her mother, she heads below deck. Despite its smothering walls and stale smells, the Oasis is the only safe harbor they have.

As they head downstairs, Amity tries to find the smile that felt so enduring not that long ago, but it feels long gone.

What if Magnus doesn't pass the Proving?

What if there's something wrong with the pteropods?

Amity follows her mother to the small room they use for water testing. Right now, she needs to tap into her steadfast well of hope.

Suddenly, everything within the Oasis feels like the world beyond it.

Fragile and unpredictable.

MAGNUS

*L*eaving the testing rooms after seven days must be how a butterfly feels leaving a cocoon.

It can sense the world is going to be different, it just doesn't know how. It knows it's changed but has yet to learn how.

The others who went through the testing with Magnus mill around. Some are pacing, several are compulsively rubbing the backs of their hands missing the bracelets they've worn all their lives so they can access the doors of the Oasis. Maybe it's because the chip that decides their future is about to be inserted.

One or two are like Magnus, standing still, knowing no amount of pacing is going to get rid of the edgy tension.

Someone comes to stand beside him, the flash of red hair telling Magnus who it is even before he speaks. "Glad that's over."

It's Dean, Ronan's younger brother who just spent seven days going through the testing with him. Magnus tries to smile, wishing relief was something he was feeling. "In some ways, it's only just started."

Dean rubs his chin. "Depends what's in the box, doesn't it?" He nudges Magnus. "Or what's not in the box."

"Technically, it's decided the moment that chip is inserted in your hand."

The door at the other end of the room opens and everyone stops. Elena, one of the High Bound, is standing on the other side. She smiles calmly. "It's time."

Magnus's pulse rockets for the moon.

Despite wanting to rush to the front, Magnus falls into the line that forms down the room, finding himself at the end. Almost wishing he'd paced more, he doesn't object. Bounds don't take before others.

If he's Bound...

His heart is pounding so hard he wonders how the room isn't shaking with the force of it. The line steadily moves forward, and Magnus watches as each person steps into the next room. The door closes, swallowing them, intending on spitting them into their chosen future on the other side.

Dean leans back, whispering over his shoulder. "You think it hurts?"

"Probably."

Anaesthetic is a sparse commodity. There's no way they'd use it for something as trivial as the insertion of a chip.

Dean shuffles forward another step as someone else enters the room. The door closing echoes through Magnus's chest.

"Surely there's got to be another way."

Magnus's lips tighten as he too, takes another step closer to his destiny. "We can't confuse Bound and Unbound. It's too important."

Dean doesn't respond, and Magnus wonders what he's thinking. Doesn't he realize that the world they live in calls for tough decisions? That the want of one isn't enough against the need of something so much bigger than them?

Magnus isn't sure how long it takes for Dean to be at the

head of the line, but it feels like days have passed. Finally, the door opens, with Elena still smiling calmly as she greets the next life that's about to be molded.

Dean glances over his shoulder at Magnus, yanking up a grin. The smile is supposed to be cocky, but it trembles as it falls away.

Magnus nods as he clasps Dean's shoulder. "May the Proving serve you well."

Dean swallows, his Adam's apple bobbing in his throat, then strides into the room. Elena closes the door softly behind him.

May the Proving serve you well.

It's the blessing his father voiced as they'd walked to the lab. It's the words his mother whispered as she held him tight. It's the words Callix seemed to stumble over before they'd all walked away.

Magnus had noticed Callix's avoidance of eye contact. He put it down to the fact they'd agreed they wouldn't talk of what happened with the Remnant. Their father would be furious if he discovered Callix almost let one step onto the shores of Askala. With the Remnant dispatched, silence seemed the best option. The strain of the secret must be why it feels like Callix has been avoiding him...and why those words were so hard for him to say.

Everyone going through the Proving has those words said to them. Most people want to be Bound. Despite the responsibility, it means a right to have children. But not everyone is entitled to such a gift. Only those who deserve to inherit the earth hold that right.

The door opens, Elena's smile at the ready to greet him. Magnus doesn't look back as he steps through. He's dreaded and anticipated this moment for years. He's wanted it since he learned of their society as a small boy, of their duty to heal so much destruction.

He's ached for it from the moment he fell in love with Amity.

The room is bare apart from a small table to the left. Elena walks over, pulling back a slip of material. On it sits a small, black square.

His chip.

The one programmed with his results.

Elena lifts it up and holds it out to him. "Take this to the next room."

Magnus nods, his throat too dry to speak. The black chip is tiny, the size of a fingernail, but it sits heavy in his palm.

Elena walks to the door on the opposite side of the room and opens it. "It will be inserted in here."

Magnus nods again, pulling out a croaky, "Thank you."

Elena's smile relaxes, making Magnus wonder if she's as calm as she seems. "No need, Magnus."

Magnus steps through and she closes the door behind him, taking away the chance to ask what she meant. Was she being polite, as all Bound are? Or did she mean something more than that? Was she trying to let him know there's nothing to worry about?

Shaking his head, he tries to calm himself. Elena may not even know which chip he has, the results of the testing are so secret. Only a few High Bound are privy to that information.

Everyone else finds out at the Announcement ceremony.

The room is empty apart from a large white machine sitting in the center. Cautiously, Magnus approaches it. There's a hole in the front, like the mouth of a cave, the outline of a hand printed on a clear, flat surface below it.

He glances at the chip resting in his palm. What's he supposed to do with it?

A green light flashes on top of the machine and Magnus looks around. They must be watching him. Glancing back, he sees the light is above a small square slot. One exactly the shape of his chip.

Swallowing hard, Magnus lifts the chip, working hard to

hold his hand steady. If his father is watching this, he wants to make him proud.

The chip slides in smoothly and the machine hums.

Now, the outline of the hand pulses with light. His heart beating heavily in his chest, Magnus slowly lifts his own hand.

This is it.

He's about to be Bound...or Unbound.

The trembling is only slight as he places his hand on the clear surface, spreading his fingers. There's a gentle whirr and his hand is pulled forward and disappears into the belly of the machine.

Magnus feels a puff of air over the back of his hand and there's a pause. He braces himself, but the sting as the chip is inserted still makes him jump.

A moment later, his hand slides back out.

Magnus glances at it, seeing nothing more than a small prick where his skin was pierced. Wriggling his fingers, he tries to absorb what just happened.

Is the chemical reaction that would make him a sterile Unbound already happening? Is his future destined to live away from his parents and brother on one of the upper levels of the Oasis?

Away from Amity?

The door on the other side of the room opens, and Magnus walks through in a daze. He scans his body, trying to sense whether anything is different, but he just feels numb.

Sweet Terra, is that the effect of the chemical?

Magnus finds himself outside, those who went before him already there. He squints. The sunlight feels too bright. The world feels too unforgiving. He thought he was ready for this, but now that the chip is resting beneath his skin, he's not so sure.

What if he's Unbound?

Dean holds up his fist, the back of his hand toward Magnus. "Didn't hurt too much."

Magnus shakes his head. "No, it didn't."

It's the pain that he could be facing that has Magnus full of dread.

Magnus looks around. They're all there, each with a chip embedded in their body. Right now, there's no way to tell who is Bound and who is Unbound. The difference is designed to be subtle, little more than an invisible chip. Although the outcome is significant, everyone should still be seen as equals at Askala, which means everyone gets a chip.

Dean nudges Magnus with his elbow. "Off to the Announcement now."

Magnus can't figure out how Dean is taking this so casually. Does he not care if he's Bound or Unbound?

The walk to the Oasis isn't a long one, but Magnus's body is wound so tight by the time he gets there, he's worried he's about to snap in half. Single file, they make their way through to the ballroom. Anyone who wants to come will be there. All of the Bounds, some curious Unbounds, his family.

Amity.

He swallows. He hasn't given much thought beyond this defining moment, but today isn't just any old Announcement. More than just his future will be decided.

Magnus walks through and finds himself on the stage. The ballroom is an expansive space, a tribute to the world of excess that used to be. A fractured chandelier tries desperately to shine up above, while the frayed carpet has long lost its shades of emerald and burgundy.

Before him is a crowd of people, all standing and hushed and serious. He finds his father easily as he's standing at the front, tall and regal like a High Bound should be. He doesn't acknowledge Magnus, but he didn't expect him to. Fairness is a quality every High Bound upholds.

Magnus keeps scanning, knowing there's one face he's really looking for. He finds her only a few steps behind the High Bound. Their gazes lock and Magnus almost smiles as she tucks a stray lock behind her ear. She's almost as nervous as he is.

The thought warms his chest, loosening it when he wondered if he'd ever be able to relax again.

A row of pedestals each hold a small box made from the timber of the varnish tree—a species so invasive, it supplies most of the colony's wood. There are carvings of the tree on the outside of the box, the roots twisting around each other in intricate patterns.

Magnus steps up to the closest one to him. He looks down at it. *This box holds my future.* He stares at it, fascinated by it, petrified of it.

Around him, he hears a cheer. The first person in line must've opened their box, but Magnus doesn't look. It's like the box has mesmerized him.

He wants to open it now.

He never wants to know what's inside.

Magnus's heartbeat muffles everything. Through the fog, he hears more cheers as another box is opened. Then another. And another.

"Holy Terra."

Dean's muttered words snap Magnus out of his daze. Dean is up next.

With a trembling hand, Dean swipes his chip over the lid of the box and it pops open. He lifts the lid quickly, face tense.

A split-second later, he lets out a pent-up sigh. Squaring his shoulders, he holds it up so the crowd can see the contents.

Magnus's father nods. "Dean, you are Unbound. You are now free to live your life as you choose, knowing you will always be cared for."

The cheers fill the room again. They're always the same, Bound or Unbound, for both are seen as a gift. An empty box represents freedom from responsibility. A ring represents binding yourself to the most important duty of all.

Saving earth.

Dean steps back, his empty box clutched in his hand, his shoulders squared. Magnus's gut clenches. He's probably already sterile.

But he'll get to live a life free of servitude and responsibility. He'll be fed and clothed, cared for over the remaining years of his natural life. Some people even hope to be Unbound.

There's no spotlight in the ballroom, but Magnus suddenly feels like one just got turned on him. It's his turn. He's about to find out what his future will look like.

Magnus knows that when he scans the box, it will open one of two compartments. One holds a ring.

The second is empty.

A rushing sound like the angry ocean not far away fills Magnus's ears. He lifts his hand, turns it over and brushes it across the lid. A faint click slams through him.

The lid pops open an inch, then sits there. Waiting to be raised.

As if in slow motion, he watches his hand grip the carved surface, then lift it. Inch by inch, it reveals the contents.

Inside, nestled on a cushion, is a ring.

Fashioned from the finest roots of the mangrove pine, three strands weave together. Then dipped in zinc, it shines with gentle strength.

Disbelief floods him, closely chased by sweet joy. He removes it and slips it onto the fourth finger of his left hand. It feels good.

It feels right.

It feels like it's meant to be.

"Magnus. You are now Bound to Earth. She is your responsibility to care for and protect."

Like he's holding a trophy, Magnus raises his left hand into the air, his open palm facing the crowd.

Another cheer fills the room, but this one feels different.

This one is just for him.

This one has tears trickling down Amity's cheeks.

The roar fades away, the room disappears. It's just Magnus and the girl he's loved for as long as he can remember.

In contrast to the wetness shining on her smooth skin, Amity smiles. A soft smile. A gentle smile. A smile that feels like it starts in her heart.

Except there's no time to talk about it. To see if the smile she's giving him means everything he hopes it does.

Because this year's Proving is a special one. And what's about to happen has every Bound here holding their breath.

CALLIX

*C*allix forces a smile to his face as he holds up the palm of his left hand, alongside the other Bounds at the Announcement ceremony. His silver ring catches the light that's bouncing off one of the crystals in the ancient chandelier and he reminds himself that his ring represents his duty to the Earth, not his tie to any of the other Bounds.

Never before, has he felt so alone.

Amity has tears streaming down her face as she stands beside him, her eyes glued to one person as he steps down from the stage. So focused is Magnus on Amity that he almost trips on the last step. *Almost.* Of course, he didn't. His handsomeness keeps him standing tall.

"I knew he'd become Bound," Callix says, trying to keep the bitterness from creeping into his voice, but knowing he's failed. It doesn't matter, anyway. Amity isn't listening.

He can see his mother standing near the front of the stage, trying to get Magnus's attention, not yet realizing it's a lost cause. He's happy for her. If that small wooden box Magnus had opened hadn't held a ring, it would have been devastating. Not that she'd have shown it, of course. She'd have accepted the decision, her unwavering belief in the system so strong it would've overridden her grief at the loss of her youngest child.

Callix looks at the faces of the other women standing in the front row of the crowd, a few of whom are facing exactly that situation, having just witnessed their child be declared Unbound. Some of them have tears through their brave smiles, just like Amity's, only for a very different reason. Their child is to be relocated to a cabin on the upper levels of the Oasis. Free to live in peace, but their genes not deemed worthy enough to be passed down. They'll be fed, but with food that fills them rather than nourishes them. Given medical attention that makes them comfortable but doesn't extend their life. No resources can be wasted on an Unbound that could be used to give a Bound strength.

Callix has heard the stories of what goes on in the Unbound levels of the Oasis. He's witnessed some of it with his own eyes. Wild parties fueled by contraband kept hidden underneath beds, the Unbound fill their remaining carefree days with behavior that looks both reckless and... well, a little intriguing.

Magnus would've been very happy up there with his books for company...

Callix knows this isn't true. Because the thing that makes Magnus truly happy, apart from the thought of saving this fragile planet, is the exact same thing that makes Callix happy. The problem is that she can only continue to make one of them happy in the future.

And it's clear she's made her choice.

Magnus approaches, and Callix leaves Amity's side, unable to bear witness to their joy. He can congratulate Magnus later, when he's been able to clear enough jealousy from his mouth to find the words.

Callix stands off to the side, alone, waiting for his father to take the stage and begin the Selection. Every twenty years, the High Bound must pass their responsibilities onto the next generation. It's important that decisions for the future will be made by those who'll actually be living in it.

Any Bound who's passed a Proving in that time is part of the Selection, those with the top ten scores making it through. Chances of Selection are slim. Only the most exceptional of the exceptional are chosen, and Callix doesn't expect to make it. He's prepared to bet someone else will, though...

Chancing a glance at Magnus, he quickly looks away when he sees Amity beside Magnus, their joy pulsing out in waves across the ballroom.

He blanches.

"Hi, Callix."

It takes him a moment to realize that someone has spoken to him, despite the use of his name. A plain-looking girl is standing next to him. He remembers her from his Proving but struggles to bring her name to mind.

"Hi, umm..." *Mary? Marcey?*

A flush crosses her cheeks and she dips her eyes. "It's Mercy."

"Sorry. Of course. Mercy." He glances down at her left hand, unable to remember if she was made Bound at their Proving and sees she's wearing a ring. So, she'll be in the Selection, too.

"You have a good chance," she says, pointing to his father, who's now taken the stage as a hush spreads across the crowd.

He nods politely. This girl doesn't know the first thing about him. How would she know what kind of chance he has? Just because he's the son of a High Bound, doesn't guarantee his Selection.

A red-headed guy he also recognizes from his Proving slides through the crowd to stand beside Mercy. Damn it! He's forgotten his name, too. The guy slips an arm around Mercy's shoulder, nodding at Callix as he stakes his claim.

Callix steps back, not wanting a fight over a prize he has no interest in winning.

"It's time for the Selection." His father's voice bounces off the walls of the ballroom. "For the old to pass responsibility for the future of our planet to the next generation. I now call upon all the Bounds eligible for High Bound status to please move to the front."

There's a re-shuffling as the Unbound move to the back, along with any Bound who've been through the Selection before. The retiring High Bound step up onto the stage to stand beside Callix's father, forming a line. Each one of them is holding a small wooden box, similar to the one that Magnus just opened.

Except, these ones only have one compartment.

An orderly line forms at one end of the stage and one by one the eligible Bounds step up onto the stage, ready to scan their chip over one of the boxes. If it opens, they've been Selected and will replace their silver ring with one made from gold, a symbol that as a High Bound, they're also precious and rare.

There's a hum of excitement as the process begins.

Mercy leaves Callix's side with an apologetic glance, as her red-headed Bound leads her to the end of the line. Magnus is nearing the stage with Amity in front of him. Callix takes up his position as the very last person in line, needing time to regroup before the eyes of the ballroom fall upon him.

He watches as Bound after Bound unsuccessfully scan their chips, the boxes remaining firmly closed. This isn't really a surprise. It makes sense that anyone who joined the line first won't be Selected. The High Bound will be not only the most intelligent, but the most empathetic amongst them, certain to be those who allowed others to go first.

A cheer erupts as one of the eldest of the eligible Bounds waves an open box in the air. It's a female Bound. Another thing that's not a surprise. Men have always been outnumbered by women at the Selection. Callix wonders if it's the empathy or the intelligence they score higher on. Maybe it's both.

The new High Bound replaces her silver ring for gold,

putting her old ring in the box and handing it back to the retiring High Bound for her to wear as she rejoins the crowd.

As the line shuffles forward, Callix watches the new High Bound standing in the center of the stage, waiting for nine others to join her. She's smiling broadly, pleased to have been recognized in this way.

Three more Bounds are Selected in quick succession, one of them taking Callix's mother's ring. He wonders how his mother feels to step down. No doubt, she'll find it an easier transition than his father. It would be strange to be filled with so much power, only to have to pass it on to someone else.

His thoughts are broken by Amity walking onto the stage and approaching one of the remaining retiring High Bounds.

Callix swallows, steps forward in the line and finds himself shaking slightly. He knows how much this means to Amity. They'd spoken about this moment for hours at length over the years, with Amity certain Callix would be selected and him feeling the same about her. Strangely, they'd never talked about Magnus and how he'd fare.

Amity scans her hand over the top of the box and it snaps open so quickly, she doesn't even need to pry open the lid. It's as if it's the easiest decision that's ever been made. Amity was an obvious choice. There's nobody in Askala smarter or kinder than her.

He watches as Amity replaces her ring—the same ring he'd been so happy to see her receive only a year before when his future had been so different. It seems right that she's relinquishing that ring now, symbolic of her passing up the life he'd imagined they'd share together.

She joins the other High Bounds at the front of the stage, barely pausing to accept their congratulations as she's watching Magnus walk toward their father.

Callix sighs. Of course Magnus would choose their father. It means if the box opens, Callix will need to approach one of the other High Bounds. Which makes no difference to the result of course, but… as the first born son, Callix had always had the foolish dream of sharing this moment with the man he calls Dad. Just another thing Magnus is taking from him, for he's certain he's about to witness the Selection of the fifth new High Bound.

Magnus scans his hand across the box and it clicks open. The smile on their father's face is immediate and filled with pride. It's the smile of Callix's shattered dreams.

"It will all be o—," says Mercy from a few places up in the line, her voice swallowed by the cheers of the audience.

He locks his gaze on Mercy and she holds it. It's like he's seeing this strange, mouse-like girl for the first time. How could she have known that Magnus's Selection was going to feel like a dagger in his heart?

Working hard, he shifts the frown from his face, replacing it with a smile, as he claps his hands, watching Magnus join Amity at the front of the stage.

Only four more to go with at least a dozen people in front of him. He steps forward again, praying to sweet Terra he won't be Selected to spend the rest of his life making decisions while standing beside the happy couple.

Mercy's boyfriend goes next, and as Callix expects, the box he scans remains tightly closed. He shrugs dramatically, bows and leaves the stage.

Mercy doesn't seem surprised. She glances back at Callix before taking the stage, leaving him wondering why she's paying him so much attention all of a sudden.

Mercy also fails to open a box, although it seems to be the decision she expects. Her eyes return to Callix as she exits the stage at the opposite end and he nods at her.

Shaking her from his thoughts, he watches as the next three High Bounds are Selected, two females and one male, which leaves only one to go. And with only one woman in front of

Callix in the line, it doesn't take a genius to figure out it's going to be one of them.

The woman turns to Callix and shakes his hand before she steps onto the stage and he catches what he hopes is an excessive amount of empathy in her eyes. Please, let it be her. *Please.* He can't spend the rest of his life being tortured by his shattered dreams.

She walks toward the last of the retiring High Bounds remaining on the stage. It's a man named Archer. He's around the same age as Callix's father, with a jolly kind of face. He seems pleased to have the honour of handing out the final ring.

The Bound waves the back of her hand over the box. Once. Twice. Three times.

Callix can feel his heart banging underneath the thin layer of his shirt. Is it possible for these boxes to malfunction?

Archer pulls the box away and places a hand on the Bound's shoulder, gently guiding her away.

This can't be happening. Callix quickly counts the High Bounds at the front of the stage, hoping there's been an error.

Nine! There are only nine. Maybe there's another Bound who hasn't joined the line? It can't be him. The thoughts he's been having about Magnus while in line should be proof enough that he doesn't possess the empathy needed to be a High Bound.

But these scores aren't based on who he is at this moment. They're based on who he was at his Proving. And the Callix of a year ago was quite different to who he is now. That Callix believed in the power of love. That Callix believed in the system. In a world that was worth saving.

He steps onto the stage and the crowd erupts into applause. He shoots them a quick smile and a wave before approaching Archer, doing his best to appear pleased about this turn of events. Magnus whistles from the front of the stage and Amity is jumping up and down beside him, clapping her hands, oblivious to the pain she's caused him.

Archer holds out the box and once more Callix wishes it's his father standing before him, looking at him with the pride he'd showered on Magnus.

Callix scans his hand and the box clicks open. He runs a hand through his blond hair before he reaches out for it. He's shaking now as he lifts the box from Archer's hands and removes the gold ring.

What would happen if he handed it right back? Nobody in history has ever turned down a position as a High Bound. It's his duty to Askala to accept. For the very first moment since he became a Bound he sees it for what it is. He *is* Bound. Tied to his responsibility to protect the planet for the future. And as a High Bound, this responsibility multiplies. But does Askala really need him when it has his perfect brother to keep the future safe?

He removes the silver ring from his finger and places it beside the gold one in the box and for one blissful moment his hand is bare. Unbound. He's free. Archer clears his throat, raising his eyebrows at Callix.

"Come on, son," he says. "The people are waiting."

Callix lifts the gold ring from the box and slides it on. His fingers are larger than Archer's and he has to struggle to put it in place, knowing he'll need to get it adjusted later. His father's ring would've fit perfectly.

"You are High Bound," says Archer. "Bound to Askala. Bound to the future. Our planet depends on you."

Callix nods as he hands Archer the box. "I accept my duty."

He joins the other High Bounds at the opposite end of the line to where Magnus and Amity stand, scanning the crowd for the faces of his parents. He finds them near the front of the ballroom, holding each other's hands and smiling up at him. With both their children becoming High Bound, everything they'd ever hoped for has been realized. It must be the happiest day of their lives.

A direct contrast to Callix's own.

The noise level increases and the new High Bounds raise their left hands with their palms facing out. Those in the audience who are Bound do the same and a hush falls sweeps across the ballroom.

The High Bound drop their hands and turn to exit the stage, heading for a room located at the rear of the ballroom that's used for High Bound meetings.

Feeling a firm slap on his back, Callix turns to see Magnus beside him.

"Well done, big brother," says Magnus.

Amity appears on his other side and slips her hand into the crook of his arm.

"We all made it," she says.

"Congratulations to you both." Callix forces the words from his lips. "I'm very... happy for you."

Amity and Magnus glance at each other and smile widely, too drunk on love to notice the insincerity in his words.

Thankfully, there's no time to talk further now. The first High Bound meeting needs to take place immediately. The future doesn't wait for broken hearts to mend before the hands of time march forward.

They file into the boardroom, and approach a long, rectangular table.

Callix's father is waiting for them at the head of the table. He has one more responsibility before he can step down. A new leader must be chosen. Callix had somehow forgotten about this and his shoulders slump to realize that as his father's eldest son, this is likely going to be him.

Unless... surely not?

They each stand behind a chair down the length of the table.

"Congratulations High Bounds, on being Selected to ensure

the future of Askala is protected," says Callix's father. "The Bound are the most intelligent and empathetic of our people. And you are the kindest, smartest, and most empathetic of the Bound. It's a very special group of people who stand before me. But one of you must lead and I call upon you to take this seat"— he pulls out the chair in front of him—"Magnus."

Fire burns inside Callix's core. He didn't want to be leader, but… clearly, his father didn't want him to be either. Because his father was never going to choose him just because he was born first. That wouldn't be fair. His father chose the Bound who he thought would do the best job.

And that stings.

"I leave you now to lead us well," says his father, placing his hands on his son's shoulders as Magnus takes the seat at the head of the table.

He leaves the room, giving Callix the briefest of glances on his way out. Was that a sign of guilt? It's doubtful. His father would be feeling proud to have made what he felt was the right decision for the planet.

"Please take your seats," says Magnus.

They do as they're told, but before Callix can pull his chair in, Amity's mother, Kimina, bursts into the room. Her hair is wild and her normally calm demeanor is replaced with one of a woman on the edge.

"The pteropods!" she cries, raking her hands through her hair, her ring catching on one of the knots.

"What's happened?" asks Amity, rushing to her side.

"They're all…" Kimina can't bring herself to say the words, but Callix isn't sure she needs to. It's obvious by the distressed look on her face.

"They're all what?" asks Magnus.

"Dead," she says. "Every last one of them. The pteropods are dead."

MERCY

*M*ercy stands with Ronan at the back of the ballroom, having just watched the new High Bounds file into the boardroom. It's tradition to wait for them to emerge to see who steps out of the room first—their new leader.

Surely it will be Callix. She can't think of anyone else more worthy. It was during their Proving that she'd first noticed him. He'd handled each of the tests that were thrown at them with impressive creativity and thought. He's exactly the kind of leader they need. Someone who can apply some free thought to their laws, instead of blindly doing what's always been done.

She looks at Ronan beside her now and a familiar feeling of conflict swirls to life. How is it possible to both love and hate someone at the same time? She loves the man he could be—the man he often pretends to be. He saved her life. Secured her future. Makes her feel beautiful. But that's not the man he really is. She's seen what lies beneath that smile. His true self. And that's the part of him she hates. Is a Bound supposed to be capable of feeling hate?

She wonders if that's how Callix feels about Magnus. She

saw the way he'd looked at his younger brother just now, that same conflict of both love and hate clouding his mind. *This is just another reason they'd work well together if circumstances were different. She understands him like nobody else can.*

Ronan's grinning wolfishly at her and she knows exactly what he's thinking.

"Is it soon yet?" he asks.

"Soon?" She tilts her head, pretending not to understand.

"Yeah, you said we could be together soon. Now feels like soon."

Once more, she finds herself weighing up the dilemma that lies before her. *Go with Ronan now and her secret is safe? Or pursue Callix, who she's certain has noticed her at last, and risk expulsion from Askala when Ronan lets her secret out?*

"It's soon," she says, making the only choice she has. *She can't have a relationship with Callix from the other side of the bridge. Or from the bottom of the ocean.*

Ronan's eyes flare, either with happiness or victory, as he leans down and kisses her lightly. Mercy wonders if part of the reason he loves her is because she owes him so much. He's the kind of guy who thrives on power. It must've hurt him to see the High Bounds being selected and know it wasn't going to be him.

They break away at the sound of shouting as the High Bounds burst from the boardroom. Confusion ripples across the ancient ballroom. *It's too soon. The first meeting usually goes for hours, not minutes.*

Magnus is the first out, although the crowd isn't sure if this is because he's their leader or if he was just closest to the door. He doesn't stop to explain.

"What's happening?" shouts someone in the crowd.

"The pteropods," says one of the High Bounds over her shoulder as they race toward the exit. "They're dead."

"Everyone please wait here," says Magnus. "We need some space up there to sort this out."

A sudden coldness sweeps through Mercy's core. This can't be happening. The loss of the pteropods is a catastrophe. It's the only thing keeping them healthy out here. It's no wonder the High Bounds are in a panic.

She turns to Ronan to see the color has drained from his face. There's a different kind of panic racing behind his eyes. One that speaks more of guilt and fear than surprise.

Mercy's jaw falls open. "Ronan, you didn't—"

"Don't speak." He presses a finger to her lips, his pale blue eyes darting around the room.

"We have to go up there," she hisses. "You have to tell them whatever it is that—"

His fingers splay and now he's pressing his hand against her mouth.

She squirms away, not liking him using his strength against her like this.

He takes a step toward the door, his agitation clear. "I have to get out of here."

"There's nowhere to run," she says. "The best thing you can do is go up there and see what damage you've done. Maybe there's something you can do to help."

He nods and they race toward the exit, then head for the stairwell.

"You stay here." Ronan stops at the bottom of the stairs, a red flush spreading across his pale face. A sweat has broken out on his forehead and he's emitting a scent that smells very much like fear. "Wait for me in your room."

Mercy's eyes widen at the suggestion. "But—"

"This has nothing to do with you. Wait in your room." He shoves her in that direction and climbs the stairs.

Mercy stumbles but doesn't fall. She stands, staring at the stairwell, rubbing what will surely flare into a nasty bruise on her arm. How dare he tell her what to do! If he's serious about wanting to build a relationship with her, then why treat her like a child? Callix wouldn't place his hands on her like that.

Shaking her head, she takes the stairs, needing to see just what he's done. Her whole future depends on whether or not Ronan gets caught.

She stops. Stands still. And thinks. *Her whole future depends on whether or not Ronan gets caught.*

If Ronan gets away with this, nothing about her future will change. She'll be stuck by Ronan's side, having his babies. But if he were to get caught and banished from Askala, she'd be free to love Callix. She hates it that this idea excites her because it's all wrong. A Bound wouldn't stab someone in the back like that.

Although, if it's for the greater good...

Mercy continues up the stairs until she reaches the top landing, and draws in a deep breath.

She scans her hand on the sensor and pushes open the door, blinking at the mayhem around her. The new High Bounds are pacing around the pool, their faces lined with anguish. The other Bounds have kept away, as requested by Magnus. This is no surprise. If there's one thing true Bounds are, it's obedient.

Everyone is so preoccupied that nobody notices Mercy's arrival. Hoping to keep it that way, she presses her back against the wall and moves slowly.

A rotten smell pervades the air, and Mercy clamps a hand to her nose. The pteropods are floating at the top of the tank, gray and ghostly and tangled in the phytoplankton, oblivious to the distress their untimely deaths have caused.

"They might still be good to eat," says one of the High Bounds.

Kimina shakes her head. "They could be poisonous. We don't know what killed them."

"She's right," says Magnus, taking charge once again. "Nobody is to eat any of these. It's too much of a risk."

The other High Bounds nod their heads, accepting Magnus's order in a way that makes Mercy certain he's their new leader. She grimaces, knowing how that decision must have hurt Callix. Scanning the deck, she looks for Callix, spotting him crouched at the opposite end of the pool to Magnus, staring into the water. She can almost hear the whirring of his brain as he tries to figure out how such a thing could have happened. He dips his hand into the water and glances up, seeing her watching him.

Knowing she shouldn't be up here, Mercy freezes, waiting to see if he's going to ask her to leave.

But instead, he swirls his hand in the water, returning his gaze to the disaster in front of him, and she becomes invisible once more.

Seeing Ronan hovering near the temperature gauge, Mercy crouches down behind what were once some plastic pool chairs, bolted to the deck. The seats and backs have worn away, but somehow the thick legs have withstood the test of time and stand like a row of weary soldiers. Plastic was one of humankind's most ingenious and devastating inventions.

Holding her breath, Mercy watches Ronan shuffle his feet, listening, watching, waiting for his moment. Having been assigned to work with the pteropods, nobody will question his presence here. But that doesn't mean they won't notice him doing something he's not meant to.

"What's going on?"

Mercy gasps, almost toppling over as she turns to see Callix squatting next to her behind the chair legs.

"Nothing." She knew it was too good to be true that he'd see her and ignore her presence up here. This guy is no fool.

"Nothing?" He raises his eyebrows and her stomach contracts at the thought she's breathing the same air as him. She's never been so close to him before and he's even more attractive than she'd realized. Blond hair that's been cut short

76

enough to prevent its clear desire to curl into waves, and flecks of gold in the deep blue of his irises.

"If there's something going on, you need to tell me." His voice is a whisper. "Does this have something to do with your boyfriend?"

"He's not my boyfriend." Her words are automatic, even if they're a lie. "He's... nothing."

"Interesting. So, why are you watching Mr. Nothing so closely then?"

"His name's Ronan," she says. "And I'm not sure what he's doing."

"Are you sure about that?" He shuffles a little closer as Ronan's gaze sweeps their way, and this time Mercy does begin to topple.

Callix takes her arm and steadies her, sending electrical pulses racing down her spine as she weighs up how much she should tell him. *Her whole future depends on whether or not Ronan gets caught.*

"Mercy, it's your duty as a Bound to tell me anything you know." Callix squeezes her arm gently. "Bounds don't keep secrets."

She hesitates, opens her mouth to speak, then closes it again.

"Mercy." Her name on his lips is her undoing. She can't keep a secret from a High Bound, but most of all, she can't keep a secret from Callix.

"I think he did something to the pteropods, but I don't know what." Now that she's committed to them, her words come out in a tumble. "He changed something, thinking it would increase their breeding."

Callix's brows shoot up so high they almost touch the clouds. "He's not qualified to make decisions like that!"

"I know."

"You're shaking." His hand is still on her arm, holding her steady. Thankfully, it's the opposite arm to the one that Ronan bruised. How fitting that Ronan was the one to bruise her and Callix is the one keeping her safe. It feels like a sign.

There's a shriek at the pool. "I have a live one!"

Everyone turns their heads to look at the High Bound holding out a net. Except for Mercy and Callix who return their eyes to Ronan. He takes three quick steps to the temperature gauge and removes some kind of cover, which he slips into his pocket. Then he makes a quick adjustment to the temperature dial, and steps away like nothing happened.

Callix lets go of Mercy's arm and leaps out from behind the chair.

"Stop right there!" he calls, striding toward Ronan.

Mercy stays where she is, too shocked and frightened to move. Her heart is pounding so hard she wonders if it's possible to wear itself out.

The High Bounds have looked up from the net now, all eyes on Callix.

"Stop him!" shouts Callix, pointing at Ronan, who's decided to take his chances and run toward the door.

Magnus is the first to move and he's fast. He reaches Ronan in the time it takes Mercy to draw another breath and he wrestles him to the ground.

"He has something in his pocket," says Callix, crouching down beside them.

There's a struggle, but Callix emerges with something in his hand and Magnus hauls Ronan to his feet. Another of the male High Bound helps Magnus to restrain him.

Mercy knows how strong Ronan is, but sees that he's met his match in Magnus.

Glancing at the door, Mercy considers making her own run for it, deciding against it. It would only make her look more guilty than she already is.

Although, what exactly is she guilty of? She had nothing to

do with killing those pteropods. The only thing she's guilty of here is drawing Callix's attention to Ronan.

Her whole future depends on whether or not Ronan gets caught.

She shakes those words from her head. Her actions had been for the greater good. She was behaving as any Bound would.

"It's a fake temperature gauge," says Callix, handing a square piece of plastic to Kimina. "He adjusted the temperature of the tank and covered it up with this."

Mercy gasps, although nobody hears her. They're too busy gasping themselves.

"Why would you do such a thing?" Magnus shakes his head.

The same look of fear that Mercy had seen on Ronan's face in the ballroom returns. He knows he's gone too far.

"I thought..." He looks to his feet, all fight flowing out of him. "The warmer the water, the faster the pods breed. I thought if we raised the temperature by just a couple of degrees it would increase their numbers. I thought—"

"You fool!" Kimina shakes her head, tears spilling openly down her face. "Don't you know that increasing the temperature lowers the dissolved oxygen levels? You just suffocated them! Why didn't you talk to me about your idea instead of just barging ahead? Look what you've done! It's taken us years to build up such a healthy population."

"I thought—"

"Did you work alone?" Kimina isn't interested in hearing what Ronan thinks, but her question freezes the blood in Mercy's veins. "Who else knows about this?"

"Nobody," says Ronan, a new panicked tone entering his voice. "Nobody knows."

And now Mercy realizes why he didn't want her to follow him to the pool deck. Why he'd pushed her away with such force.

He was protecting her. And he's still protecting her now. Had she been wrong about him all this time, blinded by her feelings for Callix? Was it possible his love for her stretched beyond his own selfish reasons?

She holds her breath and waits to see if Callix is going to protect her, too.

He says nothing and very slowly she lets out the breath.

"He must be banished," says Kimina, shooting a glare of pure disgust at Ronan.

"We have a lot to discuss," says Magnus. "High Bounds, let's take a break and return to the boardroom in one hour to resume our meeting. We'll decide his fate there."

"Kimina, do you need help cleaning this up?" asks Callix.

She shakes her head. "Thank you, but no. I need to take some tests and see if we have any survivors."

"And what about him?" asks the High Bound still holding Ronan by the arm.

"He can wait in the brig while his future is decided," says Magnus, referring to the small prison on the Oasis.

Mercy shudders, knowing that whatever future is decided for Ronan, it's not going to be good.

As for her own future, it really had depended on whether or not Ronan got caught. But as guilty as she feels for the part she played in that, she finds herself unable to be upset. Ronan may love her, but the truth is that she feels nothing for him other than gratitude for the part he played in securing her future as a Bound. Is gratitude enough to bind yourself to someone for the rest of your life?

She rubs at her sore arm, feeling the sting of Ronan's final touch. Then she switches hands to rub at her other arm where Callix had touched her for the first time. A touch filled with promise and hope.

No, gratitude isn't enough.

Finally, she's free to choose her own path.

AMITY

*W*atching Magnus leave is hard. As he walks away, his handsome face is marred by a frown so severe, it seems to start somewhere deep inside him. He barely notices anyone as he leaves the cruise ship, too many big decisions now weighing on his shoulders.

As he passes Amity, though, he pauses, eyes flickering her way. He opens his mouth as if to say something, then must change his mind, because he closes it again. With a look that's almost apologetic, he disappears down the stairs.

Aching to say something, Amity turns back to the pool. Her mother is standing at the edge, frozen as she stares at the tiny bodies littering the surface. Her face is ravaged with the knowledge of their deaths.

"Are you sure you don't need a hand, Mom?"

"No, honey. The water testing won't take long." She swallows. "Then we'll need to clean out the tank."

Which means scooping out the masses of dead pteropods. "Hopefully we'll find some alive."

Mom's gaze crawls up to meet Amity's, like doing that is hard work. She attempts a smile and fails. "Hopefully."

Amity's chest tightens at the pain that seems to have aged her mother in just moments. She's dedicated her life to the breeding of the pteropods. She loves maintaining the intricate balance of their world and watching their glowing bodies flourish when she gets it right. Her work has kept the people of Askala from becoming malnourished.

From dying.

And now the pteropods have been decimated. Maybe extinguished.

"Let me help you with the cleaning, then."

But her mother is already shaking her head. "I'd prefer to do it alone, Amity."

Amity hesitates. Is she protecting Amity from the compounding trauma of experiencing her mother's loss as well as her own? It's exactly what she would do. Amity tries to find some personal armor as she steps forward, reaching out to grasp her mother's hand. "I want to. I don't think you should do this alone."

The smell of the pteropod slaughter will stay in their lungs long after the cleanup. The sight of their lifeless, dull bodies floating on the surface is going to be forever branded in their memories.

"Oh, Amity. You know, I never doubted you'd be a High Bound." She leans forward to kiss Amity on her forehead. "Truly, I'd prefer to do this on my own."

Still, Amity hesitates, her gaze sliding to the dead pteropods. A High Bound would offer to do this themselves, wanting to shoulder the pain to save others. Now that she's High Bound, though, what should she do? Respect her mother's wishes, or remain and help?

Her mother studies her, no doubt watching the battle play out within her daughter. "Besides, I think Magnus might need you more."

Amity startles, her gaze flying to her mother's. "What?"

For the first time, her mother's face relaxes, finding some of the softness that has always made her so beautiful. "I noticed, daughter. Your eyes have been nowhere else. He's made you feel things no one else has."

Amity swallows. "Yes, but..."

"Love is a beautiful gift, Amity, one that should be treasured in a world where our lives are so fragile." Her mother doesn't need to glance at the carnage beside them to show exactly how fine the line between survival and death is. "I know your father assumed Callix would be your logical choice, but the heart has never followed rules. I don't think it even knows they exist."

Amity tries to find some words, any words, but they've all evaporated. Everything her mother has said is true. But surely leaving her right now is wrong? Surely it can't be that simple with Magnus?

Her mother steps back, her face full of certainty. "It would make me happy for you to choose a future filled with love, Amity. Especially today."

Amity nods, her throat tight. Staying to help her mother would be about fulfilling her own need to comfort her. They've been taught over and over that putting others' needs before your own is harder than you'd think.

"Thanks, Mom."

With a quick, tight hug, Amity dashes for the stairs. Leaving might be what her mother wants, but that doesn't make it any easier. She's almost at the door when she glances back, making sure her mother hasn't fallen apart the moment she left.

Kimina is still standing where she left her, watching Amity leave. Her shoulders are straight, her face a blossom of pride and despair.

Taking it as the blessing it is, Amity heads for the exit, her pulse rate picking up. Now she needs to find Magnus.

Her foot has just touched land when a familiar voice calls

her name. She turns to find Callix stepping from the shadows of the ship. "You're leaving?"

Amity pauses. "Yes. I need to talk to Magnus."

"Magnus left to be alone. It's what Magnus does, you know that."

"I know, but I think he's done that for a reason." One she's hoping had to do with waiting until he passed his Proving. If Magnus had feelings for her like he's suggested, then he'd believe that staying away was the right thing to do.

Until he was Bound.

Callix hesitates, then takes another step forward. "Do you remember when we'd talk about our Proving?"

Confused, Amity frowns. "Of course. We spent hours trying to second guess what would be involved."

Four tests. Seven days.

A whole future determined.

Callix chuckles, but the sound is hollow somehow. "And still, we had no idea what hit us." He pauses, seeming to be thinking hard. "And do you remember when we passed?"

Amity freezes. *No, no, no.*

Not here. Not now.

That day, that moment when he lifted her and spun her around, that's when it changed. No matter how much she willed it otherwise, that's when everything between them became different.

She takes a step away. "I need to go. Can we—"

Callix grabs Amity's hand, halting her. "Amity, I need to tell you something."

Amity's eyes slam shut. "Please don't do this, Callix," she whispers.

He drops her hand like he's just been burned. "You know, don't you?"

Amity nods, her eyes still tightly closed. How could she not? She senses emotions like some people sense the weather. After their Proving, Callix's touch had changed. His gazes had lingered. Being deliberately ignorant was the best defense mechanism she had.

For a while, she hoped the feelings would grow, that maybe her own feelings would become an extension of his.

But they hadn't.

Her heart had been waiting for her to find its other half.

Magnus.

"And it hasn't made a difference." Callix's voice is flat and hard.

Amity opens her eyes, her chest feeling like a cavity. "I'm so sorry."

She goes to reach out, knowing she can't comfort the guy who's been her best friend her whole life, but wishing she could. Except Callix jerks his hand back. "Of course you'd choose Magnus."

He spins on his heel and strides up the gangplank. Before the first tear can track down Amity's cheek, he's gone.

Amity is frozen where she stands. She never wanted to hurt Callix. She'd always admired his bright mind, respected his strength.

But she never fell in love with him.

Slowly, she turns toward the forest. She's already half in love with Magnus, but she's not sure to what extent he returns these confusing, exhilarating feelings.

But all that happened without even trying. What would it look like to explore something so instinctual, practically primal?

And how selfish is it to do that?

Amity glances back at the Oasis. There's nothing she can do for Callix. She can fake emotions about as well as she can lie—and he deserves better than that. Plus her mother wanted her to follow her heart...

It feels less like a decision, and more like giving into the inevitable.

She needs to talk to Magnus.

Amity takes a step toward the forest, then another and another, her heart beating a little faster and lighter with each one. The shadows of the trees seem to welcome her, wrapping around like a soft hug. She lets out a breath.

Watching Magnus leave was hard. Deciding to follow him was even harder.

As it turns out, finding him is easy.

He's standing by the lake, as still as the calm surface he's focused on. Amity pauses at the edge of the trees, realizing what he's contemplating.

The pteropods are gone. Their main source of nutrition.

How will Askala survive?

And as their newly chosen leader, that's a responsibility Magnus must solve.

Well, he won't do it alone.

He startles the moment she takes a step. Amity realizes he's spent so much time out here, he's undoubtedly deeply attuned to the sounds of the forest.

"Amity." Magnus breathes her name like a prayer.

She keeps walking forward and Magnus doesn't twitch a muscle. His handsome lines suddenly look like they've been carved in stone. It amplifies his angles, brings his beauty into sharp relief.

Amity stops in front of him, loving the sensation of his body so close to hers. "I didn't want you to be alone."

Magnus blinks, the first movement since she arrived. "Thank you."

"Not when this is the biggest disaster we've ever faced."

Magnus takes a step back, whatever was building between them fractured by the weight of what happened back at the Oasis. "How's your mother?"

"Hurting, but still managing to be as wise as a High Bound."

It was her mother who convinced her to come here.

Magnus's face softens. "That's Kimina." Magnus turns as he looks back over the silver surface of the water. "She would know what to do now. Any High Bound would."

Amity's chest tightens at Magnus's words. "You will too, Magnus."

Magnus's eyes drift shut. "I'm one of the youngest High Bounds there has ever been, Amity. What was Dad thinking, making me leader?"

Amity is back in front of him before the question is finished. Instinctively, she slips her hands into his.

Magnus's eyes fly open, his shocked gaze locking with hers. Before he can speak, Amity steps in close, leaving nothing but a sliver of air between them. "Even your first choice as the High Bound leader shows you're just what Askala needs."

Magnus's dark brows furrow in confusion. "I haven't made any decisions yet."

Amity shakes her head, letting a smile grace her lips. "You chose to stop and think, rather than rush in and react. You're going to be a wise leader, Magnus."

Magnus's hands tighten around hers, sparking a heat Amity's never felt before. It pulses like a heartbeat, skipping across her skin, throbbing through her veins.

Surely Magnus has to feel this, too...

His eyes darken as his gaze dips to her lips. "Amity." The word is almost a groan. "You're making it hard for me to think."

"Oh?" There's a breathlessness to Amity's voice that's new but she loves it. She's here because she hopes she'll get to hear it again a whole lot more often.

Magnus pulls in a deep breath, as if he's savoring her nearness. "Having you this close, looking at me like that, it's..."

Amity waits, hearing the yearning in Magnus's voice, but he doesn't finish. Doesn't move.

Something strikes her, yanking the breath from her lungs. "How long have you felt like this?"

Magnus swallows, his gaze full of truth and vulnerability. "My heart loved you before I knew what love was, Amity."

Sweet, delicious joy detonates through Amity. How are those words everything she's ever wanted to hear, and she hadn't known it?

"Magnus, my soul knew it was destined to be yours long before I realized it."

"Amity."

This time, her name is definitely a groan. Magnus's hands release hers then come up to cup her face. Amity sucks in a breath at the contact. His palms are rough after a life of living in their harsh world.

And yet they're soft, full of the gentleness and kindness that is Magnus.

He studies her eyes with an intensity that robs her of the ability to move. There's such power in that gaze. Such passion.

And it's all for her.

Amity does the only thing she can to capture the truth of this moment—she smiles.

The corresponding transformation of Magnus's beautiful face is almost blinding. His own lips tip up, his eyes blaze with light. It feels like their souls just became...*more*.

Their kiss is an inevitability they both welcome. Their lips touch slowly, sweetly, honoring the first time they've connected.

Sealing the promise of their words.

But as the pressure intensifies, as they glory in something that's far more powerful than either had expected, desire sparks. Passion kindles.

And suddenly, it's as if they've touched a million times before.

Their mouths explore as restless hands move, pulling each other in closer, molding body to body. Within moments, they're wrapped around each other as tightly and perfectly as the woven rings they both now wear.

Amity's moan is soft, but it startles them, physical proof that their connection is far more potent than either expected. They pull back, both panting, both smiling.

Magnus tucks a stray strand of hair behind her ear. "I've wanted to do that for a long time."

"The hair or the kiss?"

His smile does the impossible and grows. "Both."

To think this one emotion, the greatest of all those she's felt, was the one she was blind to. The realization fills Amity with wonder and hope. Her own smile softens. "I think we're going to be okay."

Magnus opens his mouth to respond, but then pauses as if something just struck him.

He steps back, tucking her hand firmly in his. His smile drops away, a look of determination hardening his features. "We will. Because I've just decided what we need to do."

Magnus doesn't elaborate as he leads them away. Amity's about to ask but stops herself. Magnus is the leader of the High Bound. She'll find out when they return to the meeting with the others.

Magnus is quiet the rest of the way back to the Oasis, but Amity doesn't mind. Her future is set to be filled with moments like the one they just had.

Right now, Askala's future is threatened. Decisions have to be made. And she has no doubt Magnus is the person to make them.

She glances at his profile. Magnus is deep in thought, his brows low, weighed down by knowledge of what's to come.

But his eyes are bright with intelligence and conviction. Then there are his lips, capable of such words and acts of tenderness.

And his hand is holding hers like he never intends on letting go.

As the Oasis comes into view, Amity straightens her shoulders, feeling ready to face this.

When she arrived she was half in love with Magnus. But now, Amity acknowledges that's no longer true.

She's breathtakingly, undeniably, completely in love with Magnus.

MAGNUS

*M*agnus looks around the table at the nine faces gazing at him expectantly, resisting the need to swallow. It's pointless anyway. His mouth is as dry as stone.

Is he ready for this?

Many of the people staring back at him are his friends. Several are older than him and are Bounds he looks up to. They're all solemn and sober. They know some of the most difficult decisions Askala has ever made are about to be faced.

His eyes fall on Callix. His brother's face is serious, almost impassive, as he stares back. Magnus's chest feels like someone just gripped it hard. Callix has never looked at him like that. His gaze flutters toward Amity before resting back on him, even more unflinching than before.

Sweet Terra. Magnus heard the casual comments made by other Bounds, even their parents, that Callix and Amity were a logical match. Those words had speared through him every time they were spoken.

But choices have been made.

Decisions have been reached.

Surely Callix will accept that their love couldn't be denied. That this is how it's meant to be.

Callix hasn't blinked as he stares back at Magnus. *He's probably waiting for me to speak.*

They all are.

Magnus looks away from his brother, and his gaze falls on Amity. It was inevitable it would find her, it's where his whole being wants to be. Her thick, black hair is swept back in its usual braid, her lips are in the same flat line that everyone else's are.

Except Magnus has touched that hair.

He's kissed those lips.

Something in Amity's eyes soften, as if she's remembering those moments, too.

Magnus's spine straightens. Their love is all the faith he needs.

He's ready for this.

"Before we make the big decisions that need to be made, I think it's best to allocate roles. We're responsible for Askala now, it would be useful to understand within what capacity."

The heads around him nod. Amity seems to pull in a breath, while Callix doesn't move.

"Callix. I think your bright mind would be a wonderful asset to the Provings. I'd like you to oversee the testing and data banks."

Magnus hopes that's a role that interests him, and being such an important one, it may lessen the sting of losing Amity.

Callix's lips tighten. "Very well."

Magnus has to work against the frown those words trigger. The stress of what's coming must be weighing heavily on Callix for him to respond like that.

Instead, he looks to the woman beside him. "Thea. Your skills would be a wonderful resource in running the infirmary."

Thea smiles. "It would be an honor, Magnus."

Working around the room, Magnus allocates roles. The gardens. The water supply. The kitchens. Overseeing the Unbounds.

Every High Bound accepts their responsibility humbly and gratefully.

Amity is the last. "Amity, like your mother, you have shown great aptitude with the pteropods. I would like to suggest you take over their care."

Amity's eyes mist over. "I will do everything possible to make my mother proud and to serve Askala as best I can."

Magnus's heart swells in his too-tight chest. Amity has just been handed one of the most challenging jobs given the disaster that just took place, and she accepted it with a smile.

Kimina gave them the news before they'd entered the room and began the meeting. Her face had been grave as she'd told them the pteropods were all dead.

None had survived, even the one they'd pulled from the tank alive.

Amity clears her throat. "We'll need to send out a team to harvest more pods."

Magnus nods. It's the first thing they'll need to coordinate. "We'll assemble the strongest of the Bounds. It's not an easy task."

Thea clasps her hands on the table. "I'll review the stock at the infirmary to make sure we're well prepared."

Which is why Magnus chose Thea for her role. Never had he met a more steadfast, organized woman. "Thank you, Thea. All going well, we won't need it, but we need to be ready for any outcome."

They all know finding pteropods is the most dangerous task the colony of Askala can face. Taking one of the dwindling liferafts from the Oasis out to sea, swimming in the acidic ocean, diving down frantically scooping up as many pods as possible, the whole time scanning for leatherskins. If they're lucky, they'll return before the boat disintegrates with enough pteropods to start a new breeding population.

A fist slams on the table, the dull thud making Thea jump. "How did this happen, Magnus?"

It's Dorian, one of the older new High Bounds. He's frowning ferociously as his beard twitches with agitation.

Magnus opens his palms as he raises them. "Ronan seemed to think he was helping."

Dorian glares at anyone who's willing to make eye contact. "That boy wasn't thinking of the greater good. This was a Bound wanting glory." Honesty has always been a point of pride for Dorian.

Magnus shakes his head. "Bounds don't seek glory. I find it hard to believe that's what Ronan was after."

Dorian harrumphs as he crosses his arms.

Magnus looks at the others, noting the disquiet on their faces. "Whatever his intent, it's the outcome that matters. As we all know, the global hothouse that we live in means everything grows quickly, leaving our food nutrient poor. The ocean is too dangerous to fish from. With the pteropods gone, our colony now has no source of nutrition until we can harvest more and breed sufficient numbers."

Thea shakes her head. "He must be banished."

Magnus's stomach clenches. Before Amity arrived by the lake, he'd already realized there's no possible way Ronan can remain in the colony after the damage he's wreaked. "As you're aware, Ronan has taken responsibility for the destruction of the pteropods. This is a serious crime with significant repercussions. Our colony must see that breaking our laws compromises our future. We shall vote. All those who decree Ronan is to be banished, raise their hands."

Like a slow-rolling wave, hands lift into the air. Amity hesitates, just as Magnus expected her to. She'd be imagining the pain her decision is going to inflict on Ronan.

The Outlands are a harsh, volatile place. He would know his survival is unlikely.

Her decision reached, Amity's hand joins the others.

Callix is last, which does surprise Magnus. Callix has always had a strong sense of what's right for Askala. Surely he can't think that Ronan should stay. Almost begrudgingly, Callix nods as his hand rises.

A weight settles in Magnus's heart. "It is unanimous. Ronan will be banished."

The High Bounds all seem to exhale simultaneously. The decision has been made, and although it's the right one, it was a painful one.

Magnus clasps his hands on the table, wishing that was all that needed to be decided here today. "In light of what has occurred, I would like to propose another action."

Nine sets of eyes look at him in surprise and Magnus feels a shiver of uncertainty skip along his skin. There's been talk of what he's about to put forward, but no one has ever proposed it for a vote.

Some Bounds felt it was too extreme. That the decision just seemed too...final.

Well, they weren't facing what they're facing now.

"Without the pteropods to feed us, the colony is going to struggle to survive."

Magnus looks around, waiting for everyone to acknowledge the truth of his words. Amity nods with the others, but the questions in her eyes have far more consequence.

What if she doesn't agree with this?

Magnus continues, knowing what he's about to say may end the love he's only just tasted. "We have a responsibility to the Bounds, they're the ones who are going to ensure this"— Magnus waves his arm to indicate the grim world they live in —"will never happen again. And we have a responsibility to the Unbounds. We've made a pledge to care for them."

95

Another round of nods flows around the room, although everyone looks cautious. Callix's eyes are slightly narrowed. They're all waiting for him to get to the point.

Magnus feels a steadiness settle over him. There's no other way. "To save the colony, we must burn the bridge."

Callix shoots to his feet. "No! You can't cut us off!"

Magnus stifles his surprise. He needs to look confident, even though the fact his brother just openly opposed him feels like an arrow through his chest. "It's not a decision I've made lightly. But we cannot afford more mouths to feed. Every Remnant who touches the soil of Askala is entitled to stay. Every one of them so far has become Unbound, meaning we must care for them. We can barely feed ourselves." Magnus looks around. "And that's the few who don't come prepared to fight, and endanger our lives just so they can take what they want. In the coming months, we may not have the strength to win the battle for Askala."

Callix places his hands on the table as he leans forward. "You'll isolate us. We'll never be able to leave."

Magnus stands, for the first time conscious that he's taller than Callix. "Why would we want to? So we can join the same people who created the world we live in? The same world where the ocean has become our enemy? Swallowing towns and cities and entire islands, corroding the skin from our bones? Where hundreds of thousands of species were made extinct so we could live in comfort?" Rage at the injustice builds within Magnus. "The same world where so much carbon was belched into the atmosphere that we'll skip an entire ice age?"

By the time he's done, Magnus is shouting as he slams his fist down on the table.

Callix grits his teeth, weathering the storm of Magnus's anger. "It will leave us vulnerable. Our existence is fragile enough as it is. You cannot cut us off."

"It will save us. Allow us to become strong."

Magnus steps back, the fight falling away like a trapdoor just opened beneath it. He's never fought with Callix before. They'd been fast friends growing up, both so proud of their heritage, so passionate about the future of Askala.

It hurts to know they're now so opposite in their views.

Magnus straightens, although his body suddenly feels heavy. "We will vote. All those who decree the bridge to the Outlands must be burnt, raise your hands."

Dorian raises his hand immediately, three others follow. Thea shakes her head, indicating she won't be voting in favor of this.

Magnus's heart pounds against his ribs. Amity's hands remain in her lap. What's more, her gaze is downcast, staring at the smooth timber of the tabletop. Silence crowds around him.

She's not going to vote?

He tries to not make this personal. He's a High Bound, their leader. This decision is about Askala. He shouldn't care whether she wants this, too.

Whether she'll side with Callix.

But he does.

Callix slowly straightens, bringing his shoulders back. A flash of something Magnus has never seen before streaks across his face but it's gone quickly, making him wonder if he imagined it. It's almost like Callix was...gloating.

Magnus feels like a leatherskin just ploughed through his chest. He realizes that deciding to suggest such a course of action was accompanied by so many assumptions.

That he was ready for this.

That he knew his brother.

That Amity would think as he does.

That this is right.

There's the scraping of a chair and Amity stands up. Slowly, but with conviction, she raises her hand into the air. The woven ring on her left hand catches the light. "Magnus is right. We have a duty to Askala. We must burn the bridge."

Callix collapses into his chair, his mouth slightly agape as he shakes his head.

Magnus turns to the girl beside him, the words coming out before he can stop them. "You're voting yes?"

Amity gazes up at him, her eyes full of love. "I hate this just as much as you do, Magnus. This isn't about us. This is about the future of Askala."

Magnus almost smiles. She gets it. Not caring what anyone thinks, Magnus takes her hand as he turns to the High Bounds. "It is decided. We will burn the bridge."

CALLIX

*C*allix looks at the bridge from the shoreline, feeling a genuine affinity for it. If that bridge were a person, it would feel exactly like he does now.

Betrayed.

Misunderstood.

Scared.

Angry.

Doomed.

It's hard to watch his brother make such a grave mistake. He'd never realized Magnus had that in him. The ability to overrule him and dismiss his views like that. He'd thought his younger brother had loved him. Maybe even respected him.

He lets out a slow breath. He'd thought a lot of things. And most of them had been wrong. So, where does that leave him now, apart from being all alone in this depressing world he's helping to create?

It's getting late in the day, but Magnus has insisted they burn the bridge immediately. Is he frightened the High Bounds might change their minds? Surely the threat of an invasion can't be his reason—he could just open the trapdoor if that were the case.

Callix blanches at the thought of that fateful night when they'd last opened it and his whole world had fallen through.

But before the bridge is burned, there's one final use for it. Ronan must be banished. Marched over the bridge and sent to live in the Outlands. Or more to the point, *sent to die.* Nobody can survive over there. Especially someone who hasn't grown up there. He doesn't stand a chance.

How does Magnus think he's going to banish people in future? Fire them out of a mythical canon, sending them sailing across to the other side of the ocean?

Calix crosses his arms and huffs. Burning this bridge is so short-sighted. A knee-jerk reaction that creates more problems than it solves. But what would he know? He might be a High Bound, but he isn't the chosen one. If his father has no faith in him, why would anyone else?

He watches Magnus now, standing on the bridge he's set on destroying. Their father is looking on with pride, his son doing the one thing he'd always wanted to do but was never brave enough. Because as much as Magnus's decision is foolish, Callix has to admit it's courageous. It seems he isn't going to be a people-pleasing leader as Callix would have expected.

Callix adds courage to the list of perfect qualities possessed by his perfect brother, pushing down the volcano of rage that's slowly erupting inside him.

He knows Magnus has noticed his anger. He must think he's jealous, but it isn't that. Well, maybe a part of it is that. But most of his anger has been born from a place of knowing that what Magnus is doing right now is wrong. *So wrong.*

If they cut themselves off from the rest of the world, then that's it.

Forever.

They can't just build another bridge and get over it, as people are so often fond of saying.

He watches the other Bounds whispering to each other. Most seem excited by what's about to take place, but some are frightened. Change is never easy, and this is about the biggest change Askala has ever seen. Magnus may have been deemed to be the smartest and kindest of them all, but is he also the wisest? Because being smart and being wise are two very different things. Perhaps Callix can develop a way to test for this in future Provings?

As much as he doesn't want to admit it, he's pleased with the job Magnus allocated him. Being in charge of the Provings is the one job he'd always wanted, mainly because he knows he'll be good at it. Maybe even great at it. And with any luck, it's the kind of job that Magnus will leave him alone to do. It will be a relief not to have to watch Magnus live the future he'd hoped he'd have for himself.

Magnus holds up his left hand, his golden ring catching the light from the setting sun and reflecting into the crowd. Callix is lined up with the other High Bounds along the shore at the entrance to the bridge. They follow Magnus's lead and raise their hands.

A hush falls over the crowd as the rest of the Bounds copy their action and Callix bites down on his tongue, resisting the urge to leap onto the bridge and say his piece. He'd had his say in the High Bound meeting and only three of the nine other people present had voted in line with him. He isn't likely to be able to spark a revolution here with anything he can say. Perhaps if he's smart, one day he can use time instead of his words.

He spots Mercy in the crowd, surprised to see her eyes aren't on him. Instead, her eyes are glued to Ronan, who's being dragged through the crowd by two of their strongest Bounds. Mercy is openly crying as she twists her hands through her hair. Are they tears of impending loss? Or guilt?

Callix swallows, aware the decision to seal Ronan's fate was a vote he'd taken part in. He'd come close to not raising his hand at all. Not for Ronan's sake. But for Mercy's. She's the only person who's treated him with any kind of respect in all of this and he'd hoped to spare her some of the grief she's experiencing now.

He'd noticed the admiration in her eyes when she looked at him. Perhaps there was even a little more than admiration there. She looked at him in the way he was certain she should be looking at her boyfriend. Or *not her boyfriend*, as she'd been quick to point out.

Remembering her keen dismissal of her relationship with Ronan tells him there's guilt mixed in with these tears, although that still leaves him feeling bad for voting in favor of banishment.

"Is this how you treat someone who was trying to help?" cries Ronan, his red hair matching the bloodstain on the back of his hand where his chip was cut out. He's no longer Bound. Not even Unbound. Ronan is a Remnant now.

He's dragged toward the bridge and Callix looks once more at Mercy, who's collapsed to her knees, her distress unable to be disguised.

But Ronan has more he wants to say. "You're supposed to be kind. What you're doing is not kind!"

His words make Callix wince.

"Looking after the greater good is kindness," Magnus reminds the crowd. "We mustn't lose sight of that. Sometimes the right decisions are also the difficult ones."

Agreement ripples through the crowd and Callix breathes a sigh. Magnus may be wrong about the bridge, but he's right about this. Banishings can be seen as harsh. It's important the people understand why they're necessary. Ronan put all their lives at risk. Everything their ancestors had worked for is now in jeopardy. He can't go unpunished.

"Please!" calls Mercy, as Ronan is forced to the bridge. "Don't do this!"

"It's okay, Mercy." Ronan straightens his back and locks his eyes on her in such a way that Callix is certain Ronan isn't aware she's the one who gave him up.

"This is wrong," she sobs.

"Be strong, Mercy." He smiles at her through his tears. "You're better than all of them put together."

Callix wonders if perhaps Ronan is right. Mercy has done nothing but surprise him ever since she demanded his attention at Magnus's Announcement. She's like no other Bound he's ever met. There's something different about her, and clearly Ronan must have noticed this, too. He may have done something stupid, but it seems he's not a total fool.

Ronan is led past Magnus until he's standing on the trapdoor. The two Bounds release him and take a step back, standing side-by-side, blocking him from running back to Askala.

Callix has seen this in other banishings and knows Ronan now has two choices. He can continue on down the bridge to the Outlands, or he can stay where he is and the order will be given to open the trapdoor. There's a third option, of course, which is to leap over the railings into the water, but the leather-skins have ensured nobody's ever made that choice.

Mercy buries her face in her hands and weeps, unable to watch the outcome.

Magnus leaves the bridge to stand beside her, helping her to her feet and putting his arm solidly around her shoulders. Callix knows that Magnus's pain at Mercy's distress is genuine. He's never liked to see anyone upset. But as Askala's new leader it seems he's going to need to get used to it. Especially if he continues to make decisions that not everybody agrees with.

But Mercy pushes away from Magnus, telling him to get his

hands off her. It's clear she needs to blame someone who isn't herself and it looks like that's going to be Magnus.

She runs to Callix, throwing herself at him, giving him no choice but to open his arms and draw her in. She fits snugly against his chest and he tightens his grip, realizing he needs the comfort just as much as she seems to.

She's trembling badly and Callix tries not to smirk at Magnus over her head. It feels good to be chosen first. Especially when Magnus is his competition.

But then Amity takes Mercy's place beside Magnus, and Callix has to look away. That competition was painful to lose. He suspects it always will be.

"It's okay, Mercy," he says into her hair, despite the fact there's nothing about this that's remotely okay. He hates that this is necessary.

"This is my fault." Her sobbing increases along with her grip around his waist.

"Shh, hush now," he says, meaning it. If the other High Bounds find out he was aware of Mercy's knowledge of Ronan's guilt, then he could be in serious trouble. As much as Mercy is reliant on his protection, he's also counting on her.

Seeming to have made his decision, Ronan walks down the bridge away from Askala, stopping on the other side of the trapdoor and turning to the crowd.

"I walk no further," he shouts. "I will stay here and you can watch me starve. I want you to see exactly what your High Bounds have voted for. Askala is a place of cruelty, not kindness. You've all been fooled."

Mercy lifts her head at this. "He doesn't know about the bridge. He doesn't know it's going to burn. He can't stay there!"

Callix has to admit he feels sorry for Ronan. This poor guy can't do anything right. He'd failed to win Mercy's heart. Failed to increase the pteropod population. And now he's about to fail at staging the final protest of his life.

"Magnus," says Callix, as a murmur bounces across the crowd. "It's not too late to change—"

But his brother turns away before he can finish his sentence and one of the Bounds hands Magnus an object Callix never thought he'd see again.

The flamethrower.

The same one they'd taken from the Remnant who Callix had almost allowed to make it safely to shore. Had Magnus kept it for this purpose? Or had it ignited this idea inside him, along with its power to produce flame?

Letting go of Mercy, Callix goes to Magnus's side, but he's not fast enough. A huge flame has burst from the end of the rifle-shaped weapon. Magnus is directing the flame above his head, his muscled arms slipping from the sleeves of his shirt as he marches down the bridge. The two Bounds guarding the bridge nod at him as they return to the safety of Askala, leaving their new leader to take charge.

"Don't do it!" cries Ronan, seeing he's been defeated.

But Magnus isn't listening. He lowers the flame and points it directly at the trapdoor, pouring heat and fire onto it until it chars and catches alight. The flame multiples as it devours the dry timber like a hungry shark, growing bigger and brighter as it stakes its claim on this ancient structure.

Glowing ribbons of light take flight to the railings and soon they're on fire too, spreading in both directions as embers leap and twirl in the breeze in a dance of deadly destruction.

Callix returns to Mercy as Magnus pours more fire onto the bridge, determined to complete the job he came here to do.

Ronan stumbles back, shielding his face, the whites of his eyes visible, even from the distance they stand apart.

"He needs to run," says Mercy, more to herself than to Callix. She's certainly not talking to Ronan, who has no hope of hearing her gentle voice over the popping and crackling of the fire.

But Ronan's voice is louder, fuelled by rage and despair.

"You haven't seen the last of me!" he calls, before turning his back on them and running down the bridge, heading for the Outlands.

But they all know his final words are a lie. They've most certainly seen the last of him. Nobody has ever returned from the Outlands. The only difference between crossing the bridge and jumping into the water is how long it takes to die. Callix wonders if the ocean may have been a smarter choice. A slow death isn't usually a good one.

Magnus returns down the bridge, his back turned to them as he uses up the last of the fuel in the flamethrower. A towering wall of heat and flames follows him. If it weren't so tragic, the sight of all those leaping flames might even be beautiful.

"For the greater good!" says Magnus, raising his left hand in the smoke-stained air.

Callix can see he's taken no joy in what he's just done, and this surprises him. He should be happy. Today was the day he got everything he wanted. *Everything* went his way. First, he was made Bound. Then High Bound. Then he became the youngest leader Askala has ever seen. Then he called two votes, both of which went in his favor. But most of all... he got Amity. The biggest prize of all.

As if on cue, Amity runs to Magnus the moment he steps on solid ground and they embrace. When they let go, Callix sees his father join them and pull his chosen son into his arms.

A wave of intense heat rushes over Callix's skin, stinging his eyes and burning his lungs. He turns back to the ocean. The bridge is properly alight now, and the cloudless sky is filling with black smoke, billowing up as if chasing the setting sun. Dozens of birds are circling, squawking in disgust at being turfed out of their nests underneath the bridge, forced to leave their chicks behind.

There have been many victims as a result of this decision. And there will be many more. Only time will tell how many. Askala has been cut off, no longer connected to the Outlands.

No way in. And more importantly...

No way out.

MERCY

*M*ercy waits a full week before seeking out Callix. The wait is partly because she knows he needs time. But mostly it's because she does. What happened at the bridge is hard to accept.

The decision to banish Ronan was harsh. But she'd be lying if she said she didn't expect that to happen when she'd told Callix what Ronan had done to the pteropods. She'd known. And she'd done it anyway. Despite trying to pretend she'd behaved like a true Bound and done it for the greater good, deep down she knows she did it for herself.

Further proof she isn't meant to be Bound.

She taps her hand on the sensor at the lab and the door rolls open. Callix has been easy to avoid given he's been here all week, burying himself in his new role. It also means he's easy to find. Callix has one year to design a set of tests to be used at the next Proving. She's already certain that with his sharp mind behind them, they'll be Askala's most ingenious tests yet.

Breathing in the clinical air of the lab, she's aware of how different it is to the decaying ship they call home. It's like the lab has been caught in some kind of time warp. This sterile smell will probably be trapped within this domed roof for the rest of time. However long that is.

Turning a corner, she heads for the control center. She hasn't been here since her own Proving a year ago, but she remembers it well. Memories of how her life changed in that fateful week are coming back to her now that's she's returned. She's still unsure if her life changed for the better. If happiness is the determining factor, then she supposes not. Or maybe just not yet.

She scans her hand again and another door opens.

Callix spins around in his chair at the sound of her arrival, turning his back to a large bank of computers. Her knees weaken at the sight of him. Part of her had hoped that in the week they'd spent apart, her infatuation would fade. But seeing him now, she knows that isn't true. Absence has only served to magnify her feelings and she has to stop herself from closing the gap between them and tracing her fingers down his beautiful face.

"Mercy." His brow furrows. "What are you doing here?"

She'd expected him to be surprised, but she'd hoped it would be the good kind. She'd been certain something had passed between them at the bridge that night. But his reaction says otherwise.

"We…" She hesitates at the door. Perhaps she should turn around? This feels like a mistake. But her desire for Callix drives her forward.

"We need…" she tries again.

"To talk?" he asks.

She likes that he knew what she'd been about to say. Her parents can read each other's minds like that and there's no doubt they were destined for each other.

"Yes, we need to talk." She plucks up the courage to take the seat beside him, drawing in the manliness of his scent. Nope, absence has done nothing to quell the whirlpool of feelings she has for this guy.

"Callix, I..." Damn it! Can't she finish a single sentence in his presence? This is humiliating. She'd been practicing what she wanted to say all morning.

"Mercy." He runs his fingers through his tousled blond hair and she tucks her hands under her legs to stop herself from reaching out to him. "I know what happened out there was hard for you, but you know we had to let Ronan go. His actions put all our lives in danger."

She nods, biting down on her bottom lip. It isn't Ronan she wants to talk about today. She has to tell Callix how she feels before it's too late. As a High Bound he'll be highly sought after by the other female Bounds. Male bounds are in short supply, but male High Bounds are even rarer. There will be women lining up to breed with him. She only has a small window of opportunity while his heart is still free. If indeed, he's released himself from the hold Amity has on him.

"Callix, I have something to tell you." Her stomach contracts as if the words are caught in there, displeased about being asked to come out.

"I already know," he says, flatly. "I figured it out."

She swallows. Had she been that obvious? She'd been certain he was so distracted by his feelings for Amity that he hadn't noticed her watching him.

"And what do you think?" she asks, praying that it's possible for someone as gorgeous as Callix to love someone with a face as plain as hers.

He sits back in his chair and crosses his arms as he studies her. "I'm not sure what to say. Or what to do."

"You don't have to do anything." She stands up and takes a step toward him, summoning all her courage. Everything in her life has been leading to this one moment. She literally has nothing left to lose. This is the moment that will haunt her forever if she lets it pass by.

Sitting down on his knee, she wraps an arm around his shoulders, fixing her eyes on his lips as she prepares to kiss him. But she doesn't get that far. Callix is recoiling in his chair like she's given him an electric shock.

"What are you doing?" He nudges her off him and she feels a deep flush race to her cheeks. "I think there's been a misunderstanding."

"Oh." She sits back down in her chair and stares at the computer bank, blinking away her tears. Her stomach swirls with regret and she realizes this moment will now haunt her forever in a completely different way. "I thought…"

"Mercy." His voice softens and he pulls his chair closer to her. "I'm sorry. You caught me by surprise. I'm not saying that I don't… well… it's just that, we need to…"

Now it's his turn to lose his words, but she can't bring herself to look at him to see what's on his face. Disgust? Remorse? Dare she hope it's… love?

"Mercy, I checked your chip." He spits out the words like they're on fire. "I need to know why you have the chip of a sixty year old man in the back of your hand. The same Bound who went missing from the vegetable garden last year."

She hears herself groan, almost as if she's exited her own body. That's how much she doesn't want to be here. He knows. Which means it's over. Everything. All over. She saw what happened to Ronan and now it's going to happen to her. It seems she does have something to lose after all—her life.

"Ronan wore the chip of the female Bound who went missing," says Callix. "I checked that, too. What on earth have you done, Mercy? Do you know how much trouble you could get in? You could be banished!"

Could be.

She blinks as she decides if she heard those words correctly. Not *will be*. Not even *must be*. There's hope in *could be*.

"Talk to me, Mercy. Tell me what you did." His face is serious but filled with concern rather than disgust. "I'll look after you, just like I did at the pteropod pool."

She slowly lifts her eyes to meet the shining blue of his. He's leaning forward, concentrating intently on her. Her heart contracts and expands as it fills with both fear and love. Everything she wants is right here in front of her and she can feel it slipping away. Feel *him* slipping away. There's nothing she can say to set this right. She did the wrong thing. He'll never be able to love her.

"You have to tell me the truth," he says. "Please."

"It was Ronan." She breaks eye contact to stare down at the floor, hating that she's ratting on Ronan again. Especially given he's not here to defend himself. Although, perhaps that makes it better, not worse. "He did it. I didn't know. Not until it was too late."

"What did he do?"

She takes in a deep breath, aware that her life is once again in Callix's hand. It's hard to know where to start.

"Just tell me what you know." His voice is calm, and she feels like she's leaping off the edge of a cliff as she decides to trust him.

"It was in the Proving." She puts a hand on her stomach, trying to still the churning. "Right after the final test. I was sitting on my bunk, upset."

She points in the direction of the lab's bunkroom where they'd slept during their Proving, although Callix knows exactly where it is.

"Why were you upset?" He sits forward, eyes glued on her.

"Because I wasn't going to pass. I pretty much stuffed up every one of those tests. I was terrible and I knew it. Ronan knew it, too. He didn't even bother to argue with me when I told him why I was crying. The thought of not being able to have a family of my own one day was destroying me. This might sound foolish, but I've always wanted to be a mother. And I was sure I was about to be made Unbound."

Callix nods. "I looked up your results. You're right. You should be Unbound."

She swallows hard as this grenade is thrown at her. Strongly suspecting something is quite different to knowing it for certain. The churning in her stomach increases and she draws in a deep breath, trying not to throw up.

"But, how did you do it?" Callix is shaking his head now. "I know our systems are less than perfect, but I didn't think they were that easy to fool."

"I told you I didn't do it," she says. "Ronan did. He was certain he'd fail, too."

"Being Unbound isn't a failure," says Callix. "The Unbounds have a good life, too. It's just different to ours."

Not wishing to argue, she lets this drop. "You know what I meant. He knew he wouldn't score high enough to become Bound."

Callix nods. "He got a far worse score than you if that means anything to you."

It doesn't. She'd already suspected that would be the case.

"I don't know why, but Ronan always loved me, ever since we were kids. We were inseparable growing up. Just like you and Am—" She winces, knowing it's too late to drag back her words.

"It's okay," he says, a hardness crossing over his eyes. "I've moved on."

Hoping that what he says is true, she continues. "He told me not to cry. Said he had everything worked out. He had two chips we could use. He handed me a small jar and told me when they gave me one at the end of the Proving I needed to switch it for the one he gave me. If I did that, everything would be okay. We'd both be made Bound and I could go on to have the child

113

I'd always wanted. Stupidly at the time, I didn't realize he meant for that child to also be his."

"How did he get the chips?" Callix wrings his hands in his lap. "Did he kill the Bounds in the garden?"

Mercy winces. "No! He didn't kill anybody. He found them, but they were already dead. I swear it. Well, I swear that's what he told me. He said they ate poison from the leaves of an oleander tree and lay down in the garden to die."

It's only as she says these words that she wonders for the first time how Ronan had known that's how they'd died. But Callix is fixated on another detail in the story.

"Why would they do that?" He's shocked, his jaw hanging down and his eyes wide. "No Bound has ever taken their own life. We have a duty to Askala."

"They already did their duty." She shakes her head at the blinkers he's wearing. "They had a daughter and raised her the best way they could, only for her to become Unbound. She had to leave them to start a new life on the upper decks. They were heartbroken."

"How do you know this?" he asks.

"Ronan told me," she says, realizing how flimsy the whole story is. "He cut the chips from their hands and buried their bodies underneath the rosemary bushes. Check if you don't believe me. Their bodies will still be there. He said the chip he gave me belonged to the woman. He said nobody would ever find out."

"Well, he mixed up the chips, just like he mixed up everything else in his life," says Callix. "And now look at the mess you're in."

"I'd be in a worse mess if I'd been made Unbound." She juts her chin and looks at him.

"The Unbounds are cared for!" His voice is raised now. Defensive. Angry. She's pushed him too far. "They'd never survive without us."

"I'm talking about having children." Her hands are drawn to her middle as she acknowledges her desire to have a baby grow in there one day. "If I'd been made Unbound..."

"Is this really a world you want to bring children into?" he asks, seeming to be regaining his control. "I'm not sure I do. But as a Bound, I must. We all have our duties, they're just different. Some people are forced to have children against their will and others are unable to when that's all they want. Both situations are just as bad as each other."

Mercy crosses her arms, not sure she agrees with this. But as she opens her mouth to reply, the door whooshes open. Both Mercy and Callix jump in their seats as if they've been caught doing something wrong. Which perhaps they have. Or at least, she has.

Magnus and Amity are standing in the doorway and Mercy notices their tightly-held hands spring apart when they see the look on Callix's face. It's obvious to everyone that he's a long way off being comfortable with seeing them together. So much for him claiming to be over her.

"Hello, Mercy." Amity's pretty face breaks into a smile. It's depressing. If that's the kind of face Callix is drawn to, then Mercy has no hope. "We didn't expect to find you here."

Magnus is smiling at Mercy, too, and she realizes they think she's here as more than just Callix's friend, which of course would take a whole lot of pressure off them.

Mercy nods at Amity, finding herself unable to meet Magnus's eye. She knows he wasn't alone in his decision to banish Ronan, but he must've led the vote. It occurs to her that she hasn't asked Callix which way he voted. Maybe it's better if she doesn't know.

"About the other night," says Magnus, no doubt remembering how she'd pushed him away when he'd tried to comfort her. "I—"

"No!" Mercy waves her hands in front of her, not wanting to

have an issue with the leader of the High Bounds. Her life is in enough danger already. "I'm the one who should apologize. I was very upset and not thinking."

"What are you doing here?" asks Callix, drawing the attention away from her. "I don't need you to check up on me. It's all under control. The systems were easy enough to get my head around."

"We wanted to let you know we've put out a call for volunteers for the pteropod collection," says Magnus.

Callix shrugs. "Okay."

"We're letting all the High Bounds know," says Magnus. "The collection is risky. There's a chance not everyone who volunteers will make it back."

"A few of our Unbound are already gravely ill." Amity tucks her hand in the crook of Magnus's arm, then remembering herself, she withdraws it. "It's a risk we need to take."

Mercy looks to the floor. So many lives are hanging in the balance. If Ronan hadn't been so foolish, none of this would be necessary.

"I'd like to run through the details with you," says Magnus. "Not now, obviously."

Callix nods. "Is that all?"

Magnus looks from Callix to Mercy then back again, smiling. "I'm happy for you, brother." He goes to Callix and thumps him on the back, then touches Mercy lightly on the shoulder before returning to Amity's side.

Mercy's confused, until she sees the pink flush staining Callix's cheeks, and she realizes Magnus is talking about her. She folds her hands in her lap and waits for Callix to correct him.

But he doesn't. And she has no idea what that means.

"See you later," says Amity, and Callix shoots her a look filled with such pain that Mercy has no idea how Amity could possibly think he's moved on.

But then Amity looks at Magnus, and Mercy realizes her love for him is what's blinding her to Callix's feelings. She's staring at Magnus like he's her entire world.

Magnus and Amity leave the room and Mercy watches the door slide closed behind them. And she's alone with Callix once more.

"Why didn't you tell them?" she asks, scarcely able to believe he'd kept her secret from his brother. Perhaps he's saving it up to tell him when she's not around. As she's discovered, it's easier to betray someone when they aren't there to witness it.

"I don't know." His voice is a whisper.

Mercy slips off her Bound ring and holds it out to him. "Replace my chip with one that will make me Unbound. Send me to the upper decks and I'll cause no trouble. But please don't send me to the Outlands. Please, Callix."

"I can't do that." He puts his hands to his head and sighs.

It's a gesture that makes her heart sink. She told him the truth and now she's going to have to pay the price.

"I trusted you," she says.

"Mercy, you did trust me." He takes her ring from the palm of her hand and twirls it in his long fingers. "There aren't too many people out here who have the same faith in me that you do. I have to say I like that."

She nods, holding her breath as she waits for him to continue.

"You know I had hopes for Amity," he says. "But she's with Magnus now and I need to find someone of my own. Someone who can love me."

"Callix, you know that I love you," she says, hope soaring in her chest once more. "I've loved you for the longest time. I don't know how anyone could choose Magnus over you."

He smiles widely at this and reaches for her left hand, holding her ring at the tip of her finger. "Mercy, I don't love

117

you. Not yet. But I think that maybe one day I could. Is that enough for you?"

She freezes, trying to decide if it's enough. Will the huge well of love she has for him be enough for both of them?

"I won't tell anyone about you," he says, waiting for her permission to slide on the ring. "I'll need to tell the High Bounds about Ronan but I can swap your chip over for a fresh one. One that's programmed to be yours, I'll alter the system to show you've had this chip since your Proving. There'll be no record of your involvement in what happened. You can be a true Bound. You can be... my Bound."

"Why would you do that, Callix?" Unexpected tears spill down her face now and she makes no effort to wipe them away. "Why would you save me?"

"Because you understand me." His voice is gentle, filling her with hope that one day love will find its way into his heart. "You'll always choose me first and be true to me. That kind of devotion is hard to find."

She flinches, thinking she understands the true reasons for his sudden interest in her. She owes him now in the same way she'd owed Ronan. She can never betray him. He already owned her heart but now he owns her soul.

It seems this is her true destiny in life. To be beholden to a man who's plucked her from ruin.

But there's no question that if it's a choice of who she'd rather be beholden to, it would be Callix. Every. Single. Time.

She nods her head and Callix slides the ring onto her finger.

"Now, come here." He holds out his arms.

She slides onto his knee and wraps her arms around his neck.

This time she doesn't need to lean in to kiss him because he reaches up and gently pulls her to him and their lips brush, then slide, then meld.

For the first time in her life, Mercy's future feels certain. She has Callix and he has her. She may not be a true Bound chosen to save the planet, but she's most definitely Bound to the man she loves.

And one day, hopefully, he'll be Bound to her, too.

AMITY

*W*hen Amity takes the time to imagine what it used to look like, the ocean becomes quite beautiful. She's seen the pictures and read the stories of millions of fish in every color. Of an ocean that was blue like the serene sky above her. No wonder so many images were captured of it—it was breathtaking.

But that was when the ocean floor was shifting sands and colorful coral. Amity's never seen coral. It was the first to disappear as the oceans acidified.

Now, the ocean floor is a vast cemetery after all the deep sea organisms sweltered and suffocated, the only legacy of their existence is a burnt red layer of sand. All that's left of that complex world is a simple food chain laced with toxic heavy metals, with ravenous leatherskins circling above.

Amity sighs as she looks away. Some days it's easier to imagine than others.

Her gaze falls on the charred remains of the bridge. A row of blackened masts jut up through the waves. Has it really only been a month since the fire tore this bridge apart? Soon enough they'll be gone, too.

Deciding to burn it had been a tough decision. In the end, the memory of the last time she was here is what tipped the balance. Amity learned what desperate souls Remnants are—she saw it when the mother threw her child over the railing.

Amity strokes her abdomen. One day, it will hold Magnus's child. Despite the challenges ahead of them, the thought trips her pulse with excitement. No matter the world they live in, their child will be a promise of a better future. It will be a child born of love, destined to forge a world ruled by heart, not greed.

And just like that mother, she'll do whatever she can to protect her child and the world he or she will live in.

Magnus was right. A difficult choice had to be made.

She startles as two arms slip around her, then instantly relaxes. It's a touch she recognizes, one she welcomes. Leaning back into the warm wall of muscle, she wraps her arms around the ones holding her.

"One day I'll hear you coming, Magnus." Even as she says it, Amity knows it's unlikely. Magnus has spent so much time in this forest he's practically a part of it.

He chuckles in her ear, sending a shiver down her spine. "You never saw me coming."

He's right. Magnus had been in love with her for years and she never realized. "But my heart and soul did."

Spinning around, Amity slides her arms around his neck. The look of devotion on Magnus's face is a familiar one, but one she'll never tire of.

Nor of the corresponding unfurling of love within herself. She pushes up on her toes and their lips brush.

How can so much emotion be contained within two human bodies? Amity presses herself against him, loving the way Magnus's arms tighten as he groans. The world falls away as she loses herself in the magic of their desire. It seems like even after a month of being together, she can still discover new feelings and sensations.

There's the shiver down her spine, the thrill that pulses right down to her toes, the throb in places she didn't know could throb.

They pull back, both panting a little. Magnus tucks a strand of Amity's hair behind her ear. "I love you, Amity."

Amity cups his face, still awed that the soul who feels things so deeply and intensely is looking at her like that. "And I love you, Magnus."

The next kiss is a sweet one, full of commitment. Amity doesn't think they'll ever stop pledging their hearts to each other.

This time when they pull back, it's with the knowledge that they need to face their responsibilities. Another meeting is scheduled shortly. They'll need to review the food stocks.

Magnus takes her hand, leading her to the shade of the trees. "They'll be back soon. I hope they managed to collect more pods than the last lot."

Amity nods. "I was hoping to catch a glimpse of them. But maybe they'll be beaching closer to the Oasis."

She can understand why they'd stay away from the charred symbol of death that remains. Ronan's death. The destruction of their last connection to the Outlands. The death of the three sickly Unbounds who've passed away without any pteropods to earn and give them the nutrients they need.

Thank goodness a second group of Bounds volunteered to go out and harvest more.

As they walk through the forest, Amity notes the way Magnus brushes the trees they pass. She doubts he's even aware he does it. It's like he's greeting close friends, maybe reassuring them that he'll care for them with the same passion he cares for her. It makes her heart smile at a time when smiles are hard to find.

Every species around them has survived because it adapted. That's what they'll need to do. Evolve. Endure.

Survive.

The corridors of the Oasis to the boardroom are quiet enough to have Amity and Magnus glance at each other. *Why is there no one around waiting for the Bounds to return with the pods?*

Magnus frowns. "They must've returned early. Maybe they were unsuccessful in finding more pods."

Amity's stomach tightens. "Maybe they found a school of them nearby."

"I hope so. Ronan's legacy is becoming more than we anticipated."

First his foolish actions destroying the pteropods. Then discovering he lied about being a Bound. Surely there can't be anything else.

From the moment they scan their chips and enter the board-room, it's obvious something is wrong. The others are there, sitting around the table, silent.

All eyes turn to Amity and Magnus as they enter, but no one smiles. Their gazes are mute with pain.

Magnus straightens. "What's happened?"

Dorian shakes his head. "She insisted we still meet. Said we need to fix this."

Amity's chest feels weighed down by the sadness in the room, but she can't find the source. She glances at Callix, looking to her best friend for answers.

But Callix looks away, a harsh reminder their relationship has changed.

That's when Amity sees Thea. She's sitting in her seat, her back looking like it's carved from stone. Amity frowns as she senses this is the source of the pain. "Thea, are you okay?"

Callix reaches across the table to clasp Thea's tightly knit hands. "They returned while you were gone." He says the words without glancing at either of them, but Amity still flinches. It hurts her to know that something so vital like her love for

Magnus is so difficult for him to accept. She's hoping his new relationship with Mercy will show him what a life-changing emotion it is.

Callix continues as if his words weren't meant to hurt. "There was a complication. Tareq didn't make it."

Amity gasps. Thea's partner! "Oh Thea." They'd only recently announced that she was pregnant.

Amity goes to wrap her arms around the frozen woman, but Thea raises her hand. "We have a meeting to complete."

"You don't need to, Thea." Magnus's voice is gentle. "We can reconvene."

The others nod, their faces soft with empathy. Tareq was a respected Bound. Talking about their diminishing food supplies can wait.

Thea's face is gray and stricken. Her only movement is the closing of her eyes as she pulls in a shuddering breath. She's holding herself together by force of will.

Her red-rimmed eyes travel to Amity's face. "I need to do this, Amity. For Tareq. For Askala."

Heart aching, Amity nods. This is why no one was comforting her, it's not what she wants. Thea needs to know she's doing her duty, despite her grief. That Tareq would be proud she honored Askala in the face of adversity.

Maybe she wants the dignity of falling apart in the privacy of her cabin.

Whatever it is, Amity knows they'll try to give it to her. Tareq has just paid the ultimate price for his people. She's lost her partner. Her child will never know its father.

Amity looks to Magnus and he nods. They won't be talking about the gardens or their food reserves today.

They've just learned burning the bridge wasn't enough to undo Ronan's damage.

Magnus clears his throat. "We need to guarantee nothing

like this ever happens again. We need to ensure an Unbound can never masquerade as a Bound."

Amity feels tears prick her eyes. If there was a way to identify Ronan as Unbound other than his chip, there'd have been no need for anybody to have gone out to sea. Tareq would still be alive.

Magnus's face is tight with tension. It's the same look he had when he proposed the burning of the bridge.

Just like last time, Amity will carefully consider whatever he's about to suggest. All the ramifications of those affected will probably have her heart pounding again, her gut will churn. Because there will be ramifications. Painful ones.

Sacrifices will have to be made.

But she has no doubt she'll reach the same conclusion, just as she did in their first meeting. Magnus is their leader. Never has she met anyone so determined to protect Earth.

"We could tattoo the Bounds," suggests Callix. "Instead of the rings."

There's silence, and a single tear trickles down Thea's frozen cheek.

Magnus shakes his head. "With what I'm proposing," he intones, his voice full of conviction. "No one will ever mistake an Unbound for a Bound again."

THE END

<u>There are four bonus chapters of BURNING.</u>

Find out what happens one year later.

Turn the page for details...

WANT TO READ MORE?

Sign up to The Thaw Chronicles newsletter and you'll receive four **bonus chapters of Burning.** Find out what happens to Amity, Magnus, Callix and Mercy one year later, and receive exclusive news and updates about the next books in the series.

Sign up at this link....

https://BookHip.com/XZZVQB

BOOK ONE - RISING

Four tests. Seven days. Nine teens.

Only the chosen shall breed.

Humans now live in a super greenhouse. Seas have risen. Oceans have acidified. And the fight for resources is deadly. To ensure nothing of this magnitude ever happens again, only those with enough intelligence and heart will earn the right to bear children and heal the earth.

Nine teens must face the tests of the Proving to decide who will be Bound to this new order. Four of them will challenge the system in ways even they can't imagine.

Nova. The gentle soul who has everything to lose.

Kian. The champion of this new world who's determined to succeed.

Dex. The one who'll learn nothing is as it seems.

Wren. The rebel who wants nothing to do with any of it.

As the fight to breed becomes a fight to survive, rules are broken, and hearts are captured. This Proving won't just decide the future of this new order, it will decide the future of humankind.

Lovers of Divergent, The Hunger Games, and The Maze Runner series will be blown away by the breathtaking new series from USA Today best-selling author Tamar Sloan and award-winning author Heidi Catherine.

Grab your copy now!

ABOUT THE AUTHORS

Tamar Sloan hasn't decided whether she's a psychologist who loves writing, or a writer with a lifelong fascination with psychology. She must have been someone pretty awesome in a previous life (past life regression indicated a Care Bear), because she gets to do both. When not reading, writing or working with teens, Tamar can be found with her husband and two children enjoying country life in their small slice of the Australian bush.

Heidi Catherine is an award-winning fantasy author and hopeless romantic. She lives in Australia, not able to decide if she prefers Melbourne or the Mornington Peninsula, so shares her time between both places. She is similarly pulled in opposing directions by her two sons and two dogs, remaining thankful she only has one husband.

MORE SERIES TO FALL IN LOVE WITH...

ALSO BY TAMAR SLOAN

Zodiac Guardians series

Prime Prophecy series

Descendants of the Gods series

ALSO BY HEIDI CATHERINE

The Kingdoms of Evernow

The Soulweaver series